'Think of the urged Marcu hand in his.

'If you agreed to relax your principles a little, only a little. One thing you may be sure of, and that is that my word is known to be my bond and I would take good care never to betray or hurt you in any way.'

'Except,' said Louise hardily, 'in the most fundamental way of all. For one thing is quite certain—any arrangement which you might wish to come to with me would not include marriage. I am not of the class of women whom m'lord Angmering, the Earl of Yardley's heir, is likely to marry.'

'Ah, but,' said Marcus, kissing her hand again—it was encouraging to note that she was not attempting to remove it from his grasp— 'm'lord Angmering, the Earl of Yardley's heir, does not wish to marry anyone of any order of women at all—either high or low—and he does not choose his *belles amies* lightly.'

A young woman disappears.
A husband is suspected of murder.
Stirring times for all the neighbourhood in

The STEEPWOOD
Scandal

Book 16

When the debauched Marquis of Sywell won
Steepwood Abbey years ago at cards, it led to the death
of the then Earl of Yardley. Now he's caused scandal
again by marrying a girl out of his class—and young
enough to be his granddaughter! After being married
only a short time, the Marchioness has disappeared,
leaving no trace of her whereabouts. There is every
expectation that yet more scandals will emerge, though
no one yet knows just how shocking they will be.

The four villages surrounding the Steepwood Abbey
estate are in turmoil, not only with the dire goings-on
at the Abbey, but also with their own affairs. Each
story in **The Steepwood Scandal** follows the mystery
behind the disappearance of the young woman, and the
individual romances of lovers connected in some way
with the intrigue.

Regency Drama
intrigue, mischief...and marriage

THE MISSING MARCHIONESS

Paula Marshall

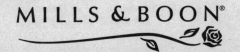

MILLS & BOON®

All the characters in this book have no existence outside the imagination of the author, and have no relation whatsoever to anyone bearing the same name or names. They are not even distantly inspired by any individual known or unknown to the author, and all the incidents are pure invention.

*First published in Great Britain 2002
Harlequin Mills & Boon Limited,
Eton House, 18-24 Paradise Road, Richmond, Surrey TW9 1SR*

© Harlequin Books S.A. 2002

Special thanks and acknowledgement are given to Paula Marshall for her contribution to The Steepwood Scandal series.

ISBN 0 263 82857 3

*Set in Times Roman 10½ on 12½ pt.
119-0702-57854*

*Printed and bound in Spain
by Litografia Rosés S.A., Barcelona*

Paula Marshall, married with three children, has had a varied life. She began her career in a large library and ended it as a university academic in charge of history. She has travelled widely, has been a swimming coach, and has appeared on *University Challenge* and *Mastermind*. She has always wanted to write, and likes her novels to be full of adventure and humour.

The Missing Marchioness features characters you will have already met in *An Unconventional Duenna*, Paula Marshall's previous novel in **The Steepwood Scandal.**

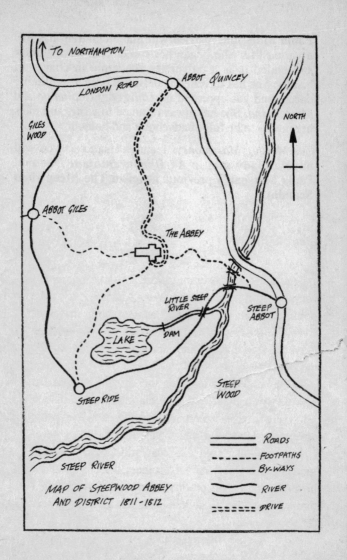

TO NORTHAMPTON

LONDON ROAD

ABBOT QUINCEY

NORTH

GILES WOOD

ABBOT GILES

THE ABBEY

LITTLE STEEP RIVER

STEEP ABBOT

LAKE

DAM

STEEP RIDE

STEEP WOOD

STEEP RIVER

ROADS

FOOTPATHS

BY-WAYS

RIVER

DRIVE

MAP OF STEEPWOOD ABBEY
AND DISTRICT 1811-1812

Chapter One

Autumn 1812

'Ho hum,' said Marcus, Lord Angmering, in his usually bluffly cheerful manner. 'Marriage, it's all a nonsense! Don't know why anyone goes in for it! Everything is much simpler with an accommodating ladybird who doesn't interfere with your life outside the one she shares with you.'

'What about an heir for the title?' drawled his new acquaintance, Jack, who claimed to be a distant relative of the vast Perceval family. 'Only possible within the law—and that means marriage.'

'Good God,' said Marcus, still in his teasing mode, 'with two younger brothers waiting to grow up there can be no problem there, so why should *I* marry? Let other men acquire a leg shackle—I prefer to be free.'

He didn't add that the lack of success of most

marriages didn't exactly offer much encouragement
to a fellow to get hitched. So far as he was concerned, all that went without saying. It was only
when he was half-foxed, as he was at the present
moment, that he indulged in such mad bursts of honesty.

Not that he often drank too much, far from it, but
he and his friends had been celebrating a marriage,
that of a fellow member of their set, Nick Cameron,
to his clever beauty, Athene Filmer.

'Everyone's getting hitched these days, never a
season like it,' Marcus continued, taking another
great gulp of port, a drink he usually avoided. 'And
now there's m'sister getting turned off at Christmas,
and you'd think that it was a coronation we were
preparing for, what with all the fuss it's creating.
Can't think why everyone's so enthusiastic about it
all, it must be catching. Well, it's not going to catch
me.'

'Care to bet on it?' drawled Jack.

'Why not? Easy pickings if I do.'

'Very well. Waiter,' Jack bellowed at a passing
flunkey, 'bring me pen, paper and ink, if you
would—and quickly, before my friend here changes
his mind.'

'No chance of that,' proclaimed Marcus, looking
down his long nose at him. Damn the fellow for
thinking that he would change his mind every time
the wind blew in another direction! He didn't know

Marcus Cleeve very well if he believed any such thing.

His tormentor was still grinning knowingly at him, as though he had a private glimpse of the future which no one else shared, when the harassed waiter arrived with his order.

'Now,' said Jack, dipping the quill in the ink pot, his grin widening as he did so, 'the only question is, how much? Five hundred guineas? To bet that you'll not marry before a year from now? The money to be handed over to me if you do?'

Marcus was not so over-set that he contemplated the possibility of throwing five hundred guineas down the drain, even if he were bound and determined to live and die a bachelor. Who knew what might happen? He wouldn't put it past his father suddenly to make his future inheritance conditional on his marrying an heiress. In fact he had half-hinted at that already, muttering something to the effect of 'It's time you settled down, Marcus. Marriage tends to steady a man.'

'Oh, I think I'm steady enough without it,' he had returned lightly, not wanting to start a discussion on the matter which might end in an argument.

So: 'A fellow isn't made of money,' he pronounced as gravely as drink would allow him to—he was to think dismally the following morning that it was only the excessive amount of alcohol he had swallowed which had caused him to throw his money about so carelessly. All in all it was a pity he hadn't fallen unconscious under the table before he had begun to brag about his fortunate state.

'It's not,' he added solemnly, 'as though I am usually a gambling man.'

'Time you began then,' announced Jack, who was one, with all the good cheer he could summon. 'Don't play the skinflint, Angmering, we all know that your pa made a fortune in India.'

'True, but I'm not my father. Make it two hundred and fifty, and leave it at that.'

He couldn't refuse to gamble out of hand—that would not be the act of a gentleman, to say nothing of a nobleman.

'Three hundred,' offered Jack hopefully. For some reason which he couldn't really have articulated, he thought that a fellow who was shouting the odds about the joys of the bachelor state so loudly might really be in grave danger of relinquishing it.

'Two hundred and fifty—or nothing,' said Marcus stubbornly, 'or else the wager's off.'

'Very well.'

Jack scrawled down the details of the bet, signed his name, and swung the paper round for Marcus to sign it, too, before handing it on to the others present who drunkenly scribbled their names as witnesses to it.

'That's that, then. Who's for the Coal Hole now?'

'Not I,' said Marcus, who had had enough of Jack for one night. 'Couldn't walk there,' and he laid his

head on the littered table and began to sleep—or
appeared to at any rate.

It wasn't totally make-believe to cut the evening
short, for an hour later the waiter who had fetched
the writing materials woke him up, helped him to
the door, and called a cab to drive him home. The
word was perhaps an exaggeration—it was merely
the house in Berkeley Square, his father's home in
London—a place which he rarely visited and where
he was always unsure of his welcome.

Once there he fell into bed and didn't rise until
noon, when his valet woke him to remind him that
he had promised to drive his sister, Sophia, to Hyde
Park later that afternoon. They had arranged to meet
the Duke of Sharnbrook, her betrothed, who was
escorting an elderly aunt there in order to meet his
fiancé and her brother for the first time.

His valet brought him breakfast in bed and a sal-
ver with a glass and a decanter on it: the decanter
was full of the hair of the dog which had bit him.
Marcus drank the port, grimacing, but that and the
food seemed to settle his stomach. He might yet
live!

Must remind myself not to go drinking again, he
told himself severely. Look where it got Sywell,
dead as a doornail and ugly with it!

Feeling much better, he decided to go downstairs
and greet the day. He doubted whether his father
would be about, and Sophia would surely soon be
readying herself to see Sharnbrook. It would be a

treat to have the house to himself, read the *Morning Post,* ring for coffee, yawn a bit and perhaps doze. He deserved a little holiday, and some peace, after setting his father's northern estates in order after the previous land agent had neglected them.

Except that when he reached the entrance hall at the bottom of the grand staircase there stood, apparently waiting for him, the most bewitching little filly he had ever seen. She had lightly curling hair of that shade of gold called guinea, which had overtones of red in it, like the metal mined in Guinea itself. Her face was *piquante* to say the least, with an impudent little nose and a mouth so sweet and kissable that Marcus was tempted, there and then, to kiss it.

She was a pocket Venus, too, the type of female which he always preferred, and was dressed with the kind of supreme simplicity which he always associated with the best of taste. Her pale green walking-dress, with its delicate lemon trim, set off her bluey-green eyes and her dashing hair. Why did one always think of hair that colour as dashing? Bluey-green eyes, too, were dashing, were they not?

A female servant stood behind her, carrying band-boxes. Other boxes were being brought in by a foot-man wearing a livery which he did not recognise. They appeared to be waiting, and none of them had seen him descending the stairs.

A guest, perhaps? Although, to his knowledge, none had been mentioned as arriving.

Overcome, and ever gallant, Marcus spoke.

'May I be of assistance, madame?'

His little Venus swung round and saw him at last. All brawny six feet of him.

'Sir? You have the advantage of me.'

Her voice was pretty, too, with an accent in it which he recognised as French. There was something about her charming face which was oddly familiar. It was as though he had seen her somewhere before, and yet he could have sworn that she must be a total stranger. He would surely have remembered such an exquisite creature.

He bowed, 'I am Marcus Angmering, at your service. The Earl's heir, as you doubtless know. And you have the advantage of me, madame. Has the butler not announced you? You ought not to be kept waiting here.'

'Very kind of you,' she murmured, 'but do not trouble yourself. The butler has just left to inform Lady Sophia and her mama that I have arrived. I am Madame Félice, the *modiste* who has the honour of dressing Lady Sophia for her wedding, and of providing her with a suitable trousseau for her honeymoon.'

Well, that explained the bandboxes, the footman and the French accent—most *modistes* of note being French. It was many years since he had been so attracted to a woman on first seeing her, and if Madame's creations matched her appearance, then Sophia was indeed fortunate in having engaged her.

What to say next? He couldn't let her walk away and out of his life without making some effort to cultivate her acquaintance further—which pompous statement, translated into simple English, really meant without him having the opportunity, at some time in the future, to persuade her to be his mistress. In even simpler words—to have her in his bed.

Marcus had read of what the French called '*coups de foudre*': that is, of being so struck by a woman on first sight that one had an instant determination to make her yours at any cost. He had always laughed at the mere notion, had prided himself on his dispassionate approach to life and love, and now, here he was in this damned uncomfortable situation.

One moment he was walking downstairs, fancy free, and before he had reached the ground a pair of fine eyes and a beautiful face had reduced him to gibbering inanity—no, had struck him dumb. The only explanation for his odd behaviour was that he had been continent for far too long. Living in the wilds of Northumberland, reserving his energies to improve his father's estates, must have taken its toll on him.

He was saved from coming out with some piece of nonsense which would have only served to convince Madame of what a numbskull he was by the arrival of Cardew, the butler, and two footmen: the latter there to carry Madame's excess bandboxes. There were enough, he would have thought, to have dressed five future brides, rather than one.

'This way, Madame Félice,' said the butler, who was now leading Madame and her retinue upstairs, passing by Marcus, who had descended to the entrance hall himself, with a 'By your leave, m'lord.'

Marcus nodded distractedly at him and at Madame, who offered him a brief bow in passing. He watched her, like a lust-struck gaby he thought afterwards, until the turn of the stairs took her out of his sight.

Madame Félice, which was not her real name, did not turn to look after the man who had examined her with such interest. She was used to being the subject of bold stares from men of all ages and every class. She had known that the man descending the stairs was Marcus Cleeve, Lord Angmering, the Earl of Yardley's son and heir. She had seen him recently in Hyde Park when she had ridden there with only a groom as an attendant.

She had recognised him immediately, despite the many years which had elapsed since they had last met when she had been a girl walking in the grounds of Steepwood Abbey. It was plain from his manner that he had not recognised her—which was not surprising, given how much she had changed. Besides, her assumed French accent alone must have been enough to have put him off the scent of her, as it were.

Given that most men of the Ton regarded a *modiste* as fair game, a cross between an actress or a barque of frailty as the saying went, it was not surprising that they thought of her as prey—or that she conducted herself as prey would, by defending herself from them in every way she could.

Oh, she knew that look in Marcus Angmering's eyes, she had seen it so often. The look which told her how much he was attracted—and which also told her that he thought she should be flattered by his attentions. She might be wronging him by thinking this, but she was sure that she was not. Life had taught her many hard lessons, and this was one which she would ignore at her peril.

For the present, she must forget him, and must concentrate instead on the business which had brought her to Cleeve House. All the same, she could not help wondering what Marcus Angmering would think if he were aware of her true name and history and what ties—even if distant ones—bound them together. How would he look at her then?

What would he say if he knew that Madame Félice had once been known as Louise Hanslope, who had married the late, unlamented Marquis of Sywell, and had then run away from him to arrive in London as a French *modiste,* society's latest fashionable dressmaker?

More to the point, what would he say if he also discovered that her true name had not been Louise Hanslope either? That she was, instead, the daughter of his father's long-dead second or third cousin— she could never remember which—and ought, more properly, to be addressed as either the Honourable Louise Cleeve, or as the Marchioness of Sywell—if she ever had the means, the opportunity and the desire of proving these remarkable facts.

If everyone had their rights she, too, would be expecting to be married to someone of her own station. In the normal course of events she would have been employing a *modiste* herself to design her trousseau, rather than be designing them for other, more fortunate women. She could not stifle an irreverent giggle at the thought of how Marcus would have reacted had she addressed him as cousin!

Stop that, Louise told herself sternly, things are as they are, and that being so I must concentrate on presenting her wardrobe to my cousin Sophia in my present incarnation of Madame Félice, society's favourite dressmaker.

'Beautiful, quite beautiful,' said Marissa, Lady Yardley, a little later, walking around her daughter, who had been carefully eased into the elegant cream wedding-dress which had been contained in one of the boxes which Marcus had seen in the hall, and who was now admiring herself before a long mirror.

'It is exactly what we wished, Sophia and I: a dress which is perfect in its simplicity. It looks even better than it did in the sketch which you showed to us when we visited your workrooms. If the rest of the trousseau is equally *comme il faut*, then we shall not regret having asked you to design it. Is not that so, Sophia?'

'Yes, Mama, but I am not at all surprised how lovely it is after seeing the beautiful clothes which Madame made for Nick Cameron's bride. The nicest thing of all is that they are so different from Athene's, because Madame has designed them to suit me rather than some imaginary perfect being in a fashion plate. I would have looked quite wrong in Athene's trousseau, as she would have looked wrong in mine, given our quite different appearance and colouring.'

'True,' said her mother. 'Madame is to be congratulated. I am looking forward to seeing Sharnbrook's face when you arrive in church.'

'Most kind of you,' said Louise, bowing her head, and accepting the compliments as gracefully as she could. 'But, m'lady, both your daughter and Miss Athene had the great good fortune to possess faces and figures which are a privilege to dress. My difficulties arise when I have to transform those who are not so lucky.'

They were standing in Sophia's bedroom, surrounded by gowns already made up, and bolts of cloth to inspect for those garments which were still to be created. As well as gowns Madame Félice was responsible for Sophia's nightwear and underwear. She had brought along samples of these as well as some pieces of outerwear, principally a long coat and a jacket like a hussar's for wearing on a cool day, which she felt sure that Sophia would also require.

When Lady Yardley had visited her workrooms Félice, or Louise as she always thought of herself, had almost decided to refuse her invitation to dress Sophia, on the excuse that she already had more work in hand than she could usefully cope with. The strain of entering a house which she might have called home, of meeting relatives who had no notion of her true identity, was almost too much for her.

And then, looking beyond Lady Yardley into a long mirror where she, too, stood reflected, she had told herself fiercely: Nothing to that. I have always stared life straight in the eye, I have never run away from anything—other than that monster Sywell— and I shall not run away from this.

Besides, who knows what might happen?

Now that she was in the Yardleys' home there was even a certain strange spice in knowing who she was, and that the assembled Cleeves were quite unaware of the cuckoo who had entered their nest. Except, of course, that she was not a cuckoo, but was as much of an honest bird as they were!

Nothing of this showed. She was discretion itself as she knelt before Sophia, pinning up her dress a little to show her pretty ankles, adding an extra discreet tuck here and there, suggesting that Lady Sophia ought to wear as little jewellery as possible.

'Yes,' nodded Lady Yardley. 'I was most impressed by the turn-out which you created for the

Tenison child's marriage. I was informed that you had vetoed her mama's wish that she should be hung about with geegaws. I, too, wish Sophia's innocence to be emphasised, not only by her white gown, but also by a lack of old-fashioned family heirlooms, bracelets, bangles and brooches. They can always be worn later when the first bloom of youth has gone.'

'Indeed,' said Louise, rising gracefully, and in the doing showing her own pretty ankles—attributes which Marcus would have admired had he been present. 'Very well put, m'lady, if I may say so.'

Careful, she warned herself, don't overdo grovelling humility. Dignified gratitude would be a better line.

This internal conversation with herself had become a habit for Louise from childhood onwards. She had had so few friends besides Athene Filmer, now Athene Cameron, that to ease her loneliness she had revived the imaginary companion of her lonely childhood, who might argue with her, but would never desert her.

Finally, everything else having been inspected and approved, Lady Yardley was measured for her new wedding outfit, something tactfully discreet as befitted the mother of the bride. Louise had already decided that it was a pleasure to dress Lady Sophia and her mama; they were not only considerate clients, but her taste and theirs coincided exactly.

Lady Yardley might not have been a beauty in

her youth, but her face had character and she had worn well, and was more attractive in middle age than many who had been called pretty when they had been girls. Louise had sometimes wondered what Lord Yardley's first wife had been like. The idle gossip which had come her way had suggested that the marriage had not been a happy one: the same idle gossip, however, credited the Earl's second marriage as having been much more successful than his first.

These were not, however, matters which she could discuss with her clients, but her interest in them was natural, considering that they were, after all, her relatives, even if that interesting fact was never to be revealed. She wondered if she would see Marcus again before she left the house. He was not a conventionally handsome man—unlike his father—but there was a suppressed power about him which Louise found interesting.

After all, what did handsomeness matter? Sywell had been a handsome man in his youth, although in his old age no one could have guessed that.

Louise did not ask herself why she might hope to see Marcus again—particularly as since her unhappy marriage to Sywell she had tended to avoid men. The one man in her life had been such a monster that it was not surprising that she had sworn never to have anything more to do with them.

Which made it all the more surprising that Marcus Angmering had made such an impression on her.

* * *

Marcus found that, contrary to his expectations, his father had not, as he usually did, left the house that morning either to go to his club or—more rarely—to visit Parliament.

He entered the library in search of the *Morning Post* to find that the Earl was there before him. Marcus could not help noticing that his father seemed frail these days. There was a transparency about him which made him appear older than his years. Nevertheless he looked up eagerly when he saw his eldest son enter.

It had been a source of unhappiness to the Earl that there had always been constraint between them: a constraint born out of his failed marriage with Marcus's mother. It had been a great relief to him that Marcus and his second wife had dealt well together. Marcus respected her because she made his father—and his household—happy. She genuinely liked Marcus, admiring in him the ruthless honesty with which he approached life.

'Ah, Angmering, I had hoped to see you,' his father began. 'There are a number of matters which I wish to discuss with you. Not business ones— I have inspected the documents and accounts which you have brought from the north, together with your report of the changes you have made to the running of the estates there. I am more than satisfied with what you have done. I should have got rid of Sansom long ago—advancing years had marred his judgement. I have nothing but admiration for what you have accomplished.

'No, what I wish to speak to you about is something more personal. I sincerely hope that you will not take amiss what I have to say to you. I know only too well how much you value your freedom, and how much the notion of marriage fails to attract you. I must, however, ask you again to consider making a suitable marriage—not only to provide yourself and the estates with an heir, but because I would wish you to find for yourself the happiness which I share with my dear Marissa. I would not like this matter to come between us, but I feel it incumbent upon me to raise it with you.'

Marcus knew how difficult his father must have found it to talk of his desire to see him married by the careful way in which he was speaking, quite unlike his usually bluff and, somewhat impulsive, straightforward manner.

He owed it to him to answer him reasonably. Of late, and particularly since he had reorganised the northern estate so satisfactorily, the stiffness which had lain between them had eased a little. Consequently Marcus's answer was as diplomatic as he could make it.

'You know, father, that I would prefer not to marry, and I believe that my wish not to do so has been reinforced by the knowledge that you now have not one, but two, other sons. Better than that, it is plain that both of them are shaping to be worthy possible inheritors of the title—'

His father interrupted him impatiently. 'That may be so, but fate can be unkind, Marcus. Of recent years I have seen families which appeared to be as well supplied with male heirs as ours lose them all to accident, or sickness, whereupon some unknown appears who has been trained to nothing and who consequently respects neither his new possessions nor his title.

'I would not wish to deprive either Edmund or Edward of the possibility of them—or one of their sons—inheriting, but I would like the bulwark of a son from you. I wish this all the more particularly since you have grown into such a responsible and sensible fellow. No, I would wish you to marry and soon. I know that I cannot compel you—but I would ask you to bring your undoubted common-sense to bear on this matter. I cannot ask fairer than that.'

Marcus bowed his head.

'Very well, sir. I will do as you wish and think about marriage. So far, I have met no one with whom I would wish to spend the rest of my life. Whatever the truth of your marriage to my mother, that to dear Marissa has been a great success, and if I could meet anyone half as worthy...' he stopped and shrugged, spreading his hands before continuing '...but so far, I have not. Were I to do so I should not hesitate to follow your wise example. I cannot say more.'

The Earl's pleasure at this conciliatory speech was manifest. He could only hope that Marcus meant what he had said.

'Excellent,' he said, 'and now I trust that you will find it possible to remain in London until we all visit Northampton to celebrate Sophia's marriage. Sharnbrook has been most obliging about the matter. I can only hope that this wretched business of Sywell's murder will not cast too great a shadow over it. I understand from a friend at the Home Office that nothing further has come to light which might give us some notion as to who was responsible. The trouble is, I understand, that there are so many who might have wished him dead, and no real evidence to suggest who, among the many, it might have been.'

Marcus frowned. He knew that some of the *on dits* which had flown around after Sywell's brutal murder had suggested that his father might be the culprit, but he could not believe that to be true. He had hoped that the real criminal might have been found, so that the *on dits* would be silent at last. Sywell's existence had been like a dark cloud hanging over the Cleeve family, and his strange, and savage, death had only served to enlarge that cloud, not disperse it.

'Two things puzzle me,' he said. 'One is that the Marchioness, his young wife, should have disappeared so completely, and the other is that the authorities should spend so much time and energy trying to discover who killed him. Given the dreadful nature of the man, his own wretched life and the misery which he caused to so many others—including you, sir—one can only wonder why they don't see his death as a merciful release for society, and all his many victims.'

'Oh,' replied the Earl, 'in these sad times when revolution and violent dissent are all around us, those who rule us do not like to think that the death of an aristocrat, even one as hateful as Sywell was, should go unpunished. As for his missing wife, I believe that they now accept that he did away with her, and that further search for her as a possible murderess is time-wasting and pointless. Besides, his death seems to have been very much a man's way of killing, not a woman's.'

Marcus shrugged his shoulders. 'I suppose that there is some truth in both your suppositions. As for his wife, until a body is found, anyone's guess about her fate is as good as everyone else's.'

'True. But since the Abbey and its remaining grounds have reverted to me, after Burneck confessed that not only was my cousin deprived of them by a foul trick, but that Sywell murdered him into the bargain, I have felt very unhappy over the fact that, if she still lives, she has been left a pauper. I would have liked to do something for her. It seems that Sywell led her the devil of a life—which is not surprising, seeing what a brute he always was.'

Later Marcus was to remember this conversation

about Sywell's missing wife and to smile a little ruefully at it. At the time he had little more to say about the Marquis and his affairs, but took the opportunity to discuss with his father some further alterations to the running of his estates before leaving to go downstairs and try to find out whether his blonde Venus had left. If she hadn't, he might contrive to find some way of speaking to her again.

From the bustle coming up the stairs it seemed that Madame Félice had not yet left but was on the point of doing so. Bandboxes, hatboxes and bolts of cloth were being carried out of the entrance hall to her carriage. She was standing to one side, supervising the operation as briskly as though she were Wellington on the field of battle.

Splendid! He must think of something convincing enough to detain her for a few moments without that something looking too obviously contrived. Fortune, however, was with him. Two footmen had just lifted out Madame Félice's remaining luggage, leaving her in the hall with her small bag, when the door was flung open and his two half-brothers shot noisily in, wrestling with one another, their protesting tutor following close behind them.

In their puppy-like play they failed to see Madame Félice, and one flailing arm caught her and knocked her against the wall. Marcus jumped down the two remaining steps, caught one boy by the ear and the other by the wrist before the tutor could either separate or reprimand them.

'Enough of that,' said Marcus grimly. 'On your knees, lads, and apologise to Madame.'

'Only if you let go of us, Mark Anthony,' exclaimed the larger of the pair. 'We were only funning and had no notion anyone was here.'

'Well, you do now. Both together and quick about it.'

'Sorry, and all that,' said the second boy cheekily on his way down to his knees, earning himself a cuff from Marcus for his easy impudence.

Louise, meanwhile, had moved away from the wall: the blow had been a light one, and the arrival of Marcus like an avenging angel was a source of amusement to her rather than relief. She knew all about boys of this age—the forewoman of the French emigré dressmaker to whom she had once been apprenticed had had three of her own. Louise had even joined them in some of their romps before she had turned from a hoyden of a girl into a young lady who realised that such romps might become dangerous.

'These,' said Marcus when both lads were on their knees before her, begging her pardon in soulful voices, 'are the Two Neds, Edward and Edmund… Like the Saxon kings after whom they are named, they have never learned to control their behaviour.'

'Mama says we're getting too old for you to call us that,' said the somewhat larger boy, Edward, who was the older of the twins by two minutes.

'True,' said Marcus, mimicking his father's favourite phrase. 'And I'm too old for you to call me Mark Anthony.'

'You are only our brother, but you discipline us as strongly as though you were our uncle,' continued Edward, still defiant.

'Oh, come on, Ned One,' said Edmund—he was always the peacemaker. 'He always stands up for us—you know he does.'

He appealed to the tutor, who had remained silent once Marcus took charge. 'And we shouldn't have been larking our way into the entrance hall, should we, Mr Wright?'

'Indeed not, Ned Two. I mean Edmund.'

'Well, seeing that there's no harm done, and that I've accepted your apologies in the spirit in which they were given,' said Louise briskly, amused by what she could plainly see was the friendly rapport which existed between Marcus and his half-brothers, 'you will allow me to leave unimpeded.'

'Only,' said Marcus gallantly, offering her his arm, 'if you will allow me to escort you to your carriage.'

What could she say to that, but 'Thank you, m'lord.' Anything else would have been churlish.

'Excellent. This way, then,' and he manoeuvred her out to where her carriage, piled high with her bandboxes and other paraphernalia, was waiting.

Once outside, though, when she lifted her small hand from his arm he took it gently into his large one, saying, 'I hope that all went well with m'sister's trousseau, madame.'

Why was she so breathless? Why was he so overwhelming? She had even faced Sywell down, so why should one admittedly large, but extremely civilised, nobleman have this peculiar effect on her?

She wanted to snatch her hand away, but reason said go slowly, lest she say, or do, more than she should. She could not believe how cool her voice sounded when she finally spoke.

'Very well, m'lord. Both your sister and her mama were very easy to please, since our tastes coincided.'

'Excellent,' Marcus said again. Something seemed to be depriving him of sensible speech but what could he say to detain her which would not sound as though he were trying to coerce her into meeting him again? Which was, of course, what he wanted to do!

'I believe that your premises are in Bond Street.'

His eyes on her were now admiring, no doubt of that. It was, perhaps, fortunate, Louise thought, that her horses suddenly grew impatient.

'It is time that I left,' she said slowly. 'I have further engagements this afternoon.'

Marcus could not help himself. 'With your husband, I suppose.'

Well, at last, here was something to which she could give a straight answer.

'No, I am not married. I am a widow,' she added.

Perhaps that would deter him from pursuing her further, since that was obviously what he wished to do.

'Not recently, I hope,' he said.

Marcus thought that for sheer banality this conversation took some beating.

Louise thought so, too. *What in the world is wrong with us?*

'Not quite,' she replied—and *what kind of an answer was that?*

Marcus released her hand, but not before kissing it.

'You will allow me to assist you into the carriage.'

Her hand out of his, Louise felt that some sustaining presence had vanished. It was an odd feeling for her, for she had grown used to being self-sufficient. The presence reappeared when he helped her up, and disappeared again when he let go of her.

She was aware, although she made no effort to look back at him, that he watched her until her carriage was out of sight. Something told her that it might not be long before she saw him again—and that something was right.

The question was, could she afford to know him?—however much she might want to. Anonymity had been her protector since the day when she had fled Steepwood Abbey, to find safety far from her tormentor, and from anyone who might remember poor little Louise Hanslope.

Marcus watched her carriage go, his mind in a

whirl. Like Louise, he could not believe the strength of his reaction to someone whom he had only just met. He must see her again, he must.

But how?

Chapter Two

'**K**now anything about a pretty little *modiste*, Madame Félice by name, do you, Gronow, old fellow?'

Marcus thought that Captain Gronow knew everything that there was to know about everybody, and he was not far wrong. It was fortunate that he, too, had been in Hyde Park that afternoon, and he had ridden over to him to pick his brains about Madame.

'Society's favourite dressmaker, has her place in Bond Street, eh? I can't say that I actually know anything—only *on dits* and suppositions which might, or might not, be true. Would that do?'

'Anything would do—better than knowing nothing at all.'

Gronow pondered a moment. He didn't ask Marcus why he wished to be informed about Madame, he thought that he knew.

'Well, she appeared out of nowhere some time

ago and was immediately able to afford not only to buy the Bond Street shop but also have it done over completely. So, the argument runs, she must have a rich backer—either here, or in Paris, since she's supposed to be French. I say supposed, because no one is sure of that, either. But who can the rich backer be, eh? No one has ever seen her with a man. She sometimes rides here in the late afternoon, but she acknowledges no one—and no one acknowledges her. A mystery, eh, what, wouldn't you say? The ladies say that she's very much a lady. Perfect manners, never presumes, unless it's to correct, very gently, provincial nobodies like the Tenison woman, Adrian Kinloch's mother-in-law—whose taste certainly needed correcting, I'm told.'

'A paragon, then,' remarked Marcus somewhat dryly. It was a little discouraging to learn that either his beauty was virtuous or that someone, rich, powerful and discreet, ran her. On the other hand, discretion of the sort which Madame was evidently practising was always to be commended.

'Lives over the shop, does she?'

'Well, even that's unknown. That ass Sandiman apparently came the heavy with her one day at her salon, and the story goes that she gave him a bloody nose for his impudence—which could argue virtue—or the appearance of it.'

Marcus was fascinated. 'She's so tiny, how in the world did she tap his claret?'

'With a poker, apparently. Poor fool wasn't expecting it, it's said. She led him on for a bit and then, when he was least expecting it, planted him a facer as good as the Game Chicken could have done—except that he don't use a poker! I'd look out if I were you, Angmering, if you've any notion of furthering your own acquaintance with her. Don't want your looks ruined for nothing!'

'Well, thanks for the warning, Gronow. Always best to know what might by lying in wait for you, eh?'

'All's fair in love and war, they say.'

'And no real notion of who might be running her? If anyone? Could the money she spent to set up her business have been some sort of a final pay-off for her, do you think?'

'No idea, old fellow, none at all. If I hear anything I'll be sure to let you know.'

A mystery woman indeed then, Madame Félice. And strong-minded, too. One might have guessed at her possessing a fiery temper with hair that colour— and such a determined little chin: he particularly admired the chin.

Marcus rode back to where his sister sat, talking to Sharnbrook—and there was a fellow worth knowing. He had to commend Sophia for her common-sense and good judgement in bringing him to heel.

Now, if he could only persuade Madame—if she were free that was—that he, Marcus, would be as good a bet as any to set up house with, then he could be as happy as Sophia without the shackles of marriage to trouble him. All that remained necessary for him was to find some means of promoting his friendship with her, and that was going to be difficult.

In the normal course of events there were a thousand ways in which he could contrive to meet a woman. If she were in society there was the park, or the ballrooms of mutual friends, or he could make a polite afternoon call. Likewise if she were in the demi-monde there were any number of recognised haunts where she might be found.

But Madame Félice was different. She belonged to neither one or the other of these two groups. She had her own legitimate business, and possibly also a circle of friends—but these would certainly not be the friends of Marcus, Lord Angmering, a member of high society, of the ton. Not that he associated much with the ton himself.

Come to think of it, he had become, except for his brief visits to London, a bit of a solitary. So he would have to devise some ploy, some trick, to further his acquaintance with Madame—which would itself serve to add a little spice to a life which he freely acknowledged had lately been rather dull.

So the afternoon found him sauntering along Bond Street trying to look innocent, although the good Lord alone could explain why he should, seeing that he was bent on seducing a woman who, for all he knew, was truly innocent. Except that in the world which Marcus inhabited, women in occupations like Madame's were rarely so. Gronow had hesitated to pass any judgement on her which was, in itself, remarkable, but that proved nothing.

In his musings he had finally reached Madame's salon with its little bow-window, a large hat on a cream-coloured shawl chastely displayed inside it— an indication of Madame's character? He sincerely hoped not.

Now to go in—but what to say? He could scarcely ask her to make him a pretty little *toilette*. On the other hand, what about a shirt? Would it be beyond Madame's talents to design a shirt for him? He could always claim that his present tailor was not sufficiently up to scratch for a man who hoped to make a good show at his sister's wedding.

Yes, that was it.

It wasn't a very convincing notion but it would have to do.

Marcus pushed the shop door open and walked in.

Louise had had a trying day. Her forewoman had contracted a light fever, and had consequently been unable to come in to work: her best cutter had thrown a fit of the tantrums on being asked to create something which she did not care for, so that Louise had been compelled to do it herself to prove that the design was not only feasible, but beautiful. This had finally brought obedience from the cutter, but having been proved wrong she had sulked for the rest of the day.

Now, to cap everything, the assistant who manned the shop counter had come in all of a fluster.

'Madame, there's a man outside who says he wants you to make him a shirt. I told him that you only design for ladies, but he won't take no for an answer, won't go away, and demands to speak to you.'

'Does he, indeed? Does this man possess a name?'

'Oh, I'm sure he does, but he hasn't given it.'

Louise heaved a great sigh. Whatever next would turn up to ruin her day?

'Very well, Charlotte. Remain here while I go and dispose of him.'

A man wanting her to make him a shirt! Whoever had heard of such a thing—and whoever could he be?

She walked determinedly into the shop—to stare at Marcus.

As seemed always to be the case, the mere sight of him was sufficient to deprive her of all common-sense.

'Oh, it's you,' she said foolishly. And then, to recover herself a little, 'I might have guessed.'

He smiled at her and, yes, he really did look rather splendid today—even more so than when she had first met him. Not that he was in the least bit con-ventionally handsome, his face was too strong for that—and his answer to her was almost what she would have expected from him.

'Might you, indeed? Am I so eccentric?' he asked her, his expression comically quizzical.

'To want me to make you a shirt, yes. Surely you must have an excellent tailor.'

'Quite so, but I wished to further my acquaintance with you, and this was the only way I could think of doing so, seeing that we are unlikely to meet socially, and I haven't the slightest idea where you live—other than it might be over your salon. As a matter of interest could you possibly make me—or create, I believe is the ladies' word—a shirt which would past muster in the best houses?'

Louise began to laugh. His expression was so charmingly impudent when he came out with this piece of flim-flam that it quite undid her determination to be severe with him. She would let him down as lightly as possible.

'Now I know that you are funning. I suppose that I might be able to do what you have just suggested—but are you really informing me that this whole light-minded conversation with me and my assistant was solely for the purpose of getting to know me better? And, if so, to what end, m'lord? I cannot believe it to be an honest one, given the difference in our rank.'

Now this was plain speaking, was it not? And he should surely not have expected anything else from her, not with hair that colour, and with her determined little chin. He would match it with plain speaking of his own.

'*You* cannot know, madame, what an extraordinary effect you have had on me. Or perhaps you can, because I find it difficult to believe that you have never attracted a man's instant admiration before.'

Nor could he know, thought Louise a trifle sadly, that her experience of the ways of men, other than those of her late, brutal husband, was non-existent. She had barely spoken to anyone of the opposite sex since she had fled Steepwood Abbey. Which was, of course, why she had no notion whether it was usual for her to feel as she did every time she met him, which was a kind of wild exhilaration which seemed to take over her whole being.

She had told herself after escaping from her prison that she would never have anything more to do with a sex which could spawn such monsters as Sywell, and here she was bandying words with one of them, and experiencing these strong frissons of excitement while she did so. What frightened her was the thought that if she were to encourage him she might find that he was no better than Sywell— or that he might even be worse.

Could she trust him?

Perhaps when he looked at her as though—

As though, what? She didn't like to think.

'Come, m'lord,' she said, and her voice was sad, all her recent light banter missing from it, 'you must

know as well as I that your intentions to me cannot
be honourable. A great gulf lies between us.'

Marcus bowed his head. He was not going to
deny that. What he could do was reassure her that
he would always treat her kindly, would never ex-
ploit her in the way in which many men exploited
their mistresses, whether they were members of the
ton, or of the *demi-monde,* that curious half-world
in the shadows which lay between high society, respectable middle classes and the honest poor.

'In terms of the society in which we live—' and
goodness, how pompous that sounded! '—you may
be right, but as between the fact that I am a man
and you are a woman who attracts me strongly that
gulf cannot exist. In other words we are Adam and
Eve, not Lord Adam and Miss Eve.'

Marcus could hardly credit what he had just
said—it was so totally unlike his normal mode of
speech—although to be fair he was being his usual
downright, honest self with her, and no one could
ever accuse *him* of being devious. Except, he
thought ruefully, when he was pretending that he
had entered her salon in order to have a shirt made—
and if that wasn't being devious, what was?

Louise must have been thinking so too, for she
primmed her mouth a little comically, and said,
'You will, however, agree, m'lord, that we have
come a long way from the days when Adam and
Eve walked the earth—and one thing is certain

about Adam, he didn't require a shirt to be made for him when he was in Paradise!'

'True,' said Marcus, bowing, and taking the opportunity to grasp her hand and plant a kiss on the palm of it for good measure. 'But I am sure that you grasp the point which I was trying to make. I would like to see more of you, Madame Félice, much more, and the only problem about that is how I can manage to do so when we do not move in the same circles.' The smile he gave her on coming out with this was a meaningful one.

'My problem, m'lord,' said Louise repressively, 'is that I do not move in any circles at all. My life is a quiet one, and I would prefer it to remain that way.'

'But think of the fun we could have,' urged Marcus, still retaining her hand in his, 'if you agreed to relax your principles a little, only a little. One thing you may be sure of, and that is that my word is known to be my bond and I would take good care never to betray or hurt you in any way.'

'Except,' said Louise hardily, 'in the most fundamental way of all. For one thing is quite certain— any arrangement which you might wish to come to with me would not include marriage. I am not of the class of women whom m'lord Angmering, the Earl of Yardley's heir, is likely to marry.'

'Ah, but,' said Marcus, kissing her hand again— it was encouraging to note that she was not attempting to remove it from his grasp—'m'lord

Angmering, the Earl of Yardley's heir, does not wish to marry anyone of any order of women at all—either high or low—and he does not choose his *belles amies* lightly.'

Why was she continuing to bandy words with him when he had made it quite plain that his intentions towards her were dishonourable? Was it that she liked the cut and thrust of argument? Or was it because, despite all, he attracted her so powerfully that the mere sight of him excited her? Nevertheless she must not allow him to persuade her to behave foolishly, so her answer to him must be a measured one.

'Ah,' she said, sighing a little, 'but you must admit that your *belles amies* are light, else they would not be your *belles amies*. No virtuous woman would agree to such an arrangement. Lowly I may be, but virtuous I intend to remain, even though it might mean that I never marry.'

'What is virtue worth,' asked Marcus, smiling seductively, 'if it prevents us from finding happiness?'

'I would not be happy if I were your mistress, m'lord, and I would deem it a favour if you released my hand. I did not give you permission to take it.'

'Certainly, but not before favouring it with yet another kiss.'

'You are impudent, sir.'

'Always when pursuing beauty,' and he kissed her hand again before slowly releasing it. 'I would not displease you by refusing such a reasonable request.'

'Then pray oblige me by agreeing to another reasonable request from me—that you leave.'

'Without placing an order for a shirt?' he asked her, his face comically sad.

Louise could not help herself. She began to laugh, recovering herself sufficiently to splutter, 'Lord Angmering, you are the outside of enough. Please, take your noble self and your unseemly offer away at once. There, is that enough to persuade you that I am serious in refusing even to consider what you obviously think to be a great honour: that I become your latest barque of frailty?'

'So, your answer is no?'

'No, no, and no again—did you expect anything else, m'lord?'

'I hoped—what did I hope?' Marcus was asking himself that question, not Louise. Faint heart, he thought, never won fair lady, and Marcus Angmering prided himself that his heart was not a faint one.

He leaned forward to look down into her beautiful eyes and tried not to drown in them. 'I must inform you,' he murmured confidentially, 'that I have a most inconvenient habit. I never take no for an answer. No, I think, challenges me more than yes.'

Louise repressed a desire to laugh again. She had hoped that her repeated refusal might persuade him to leave. She had deliberately not mounted a high horse by taking a loud moral line, since he had not attempted to attack her physically in any way, unlike

Sandiman and some others she had heard of. Other than by taking her hand and stroking and kissing it gently, that was.

'Do I understand, m'lord, that you prefer a challenge? If so, let me persuade you that I am not prepared to enter a verbal jousting match with you over whether or not I shall become your current ladybird. Had you offered me marriage my answer might still have been no, seeing that our acquaintance has been so short.'

She ended by pulling out her little fob watch and staring at it before saying, her bright eyes flashing fire, 'I calculate that our two meetings, taken together, have not lasted so much as half an hour—which must constitute some sort of achievement, seeing that it has included one improper proposal and two proper refusals. That being so, and seeing that I have a great deal of work awaiting me, I must, again, ask you to leave—and, nobleman though you are—that you will be gentleman enough to obey me.'

Marcus bowed. 'Splendid, madame. I do believe that between us we could write a Drury Lane farce which would rival Sheridan—were we not both so busy I might suggest a collaboration. That fact alone persuades me to go, bearing in mind that ''he who fights and runs away, will live to fight another day!'''

Louise could not resist murmuring back at him as

he bowed his way out, 'Oh, is that what we have been doing, m'lord, fighting?'

He turned towards her before he left and shook a finger at her, 'Address me as Angmering, if you please, not m'lord: I can see that you are not yet ready for Marcus. I shall be back, soon.'

Louise sank on to one of the chairs provided for customers, and put a hand to her hot face.

No, I am not ready for this, or for him, nor will I ever be—I think. I thought that being Sywell's wife would have affected me as cowpox is supposed to affect smallpox, as an inoculation against men—but no such thing. And what is the most surprising fact of all is that he bears no resemblance whatsoever to the handsome hero whom I used to dream about when I was poor little Louise Hanslope. The hero who would come to rescue me from penury and misery. He's certainly not handsome—but he's something better. He's not a dandy either, simply a strong man who is full of confidence in himself.

But he shall not have me for his doxy unless I truly wish it, and I have no notion what my real feelings for him are—or might be.

But she was lying to herself, and knew it. The physical pull of him was so powerful that now he had gone she found herself shivering, and what did that tell her?

Something which she did not want to know.

Marcus could not truly read his own feelings either. He had not flattered himself that Madame

Félice would succumb to him immediately, but he had been of the opinion that it might not be too difficult to win her.

He thought that no longer. There was steel there. By her appearance he might have thought her fragile. Fragile! Oh, she might look so, but she was actually as fragile as the Emperor Napoleon or one of his marshals. Send her to Spain, and Wellington would surely win his war there in short order!

On the other hand there was little pleasure in an easy conquest. His campaign to win her into his bed might be long, but it would be entertaining if this afternoon was anything to go by, and the prize he would gain at its end would be well worth winning.

To the victor the spoils—and now to return to his humdrum life again, to visit his old aunt, his mother's sister, who had arrived in London for a short stay and had written to him to say that she particularly wished to see him.

What puzzled him was what she could possibly have to say to him. He remembered meeting her once, years before, and even then, when he was little more than a child, noticing that, unlike his mother, she was no beauty. He had heard that she was married to a Norfolk squire and had had a large family: his cousins, whom, for one reason or another, he had never met.

He discovered that she was still not a beauty, but,

like his stepmother, had a face full of character. Her pleasure at meeting him was great and unaffected.

'Oh, how much you resemble your father!' she exclaimed when all the proprieties had been gone through, and they were seated together and he had accepted a glass of Madeira and some ratafia biscuits.

'I always admired him, you know, and was sad when he offered for Danielle, and not me. On the other hand I was later relieved that he had not done so, for I should not have liked to go to India, so hot and nasty, and I could not have had a better husband than my dear Robert, God bless him.'

Robert Hallowes had died some years earlier and she had been living at the Dower House on the Hallowes estate near King's Lynn. She spoke briefly of her life there, and asked Marcus about his in Northumberland.

'I suppose you knew of, if you did not mix with, that dreadful man, Sywell. He was someone to avoid, you know. His reputation was bad from the first moment he burst into society, and believe me, burst was the right word! Your father grew to dislike him intensely and there were some rumours about him and Sywell both being interested in another young woman before he met Danielle and myself in our first season. Fortunately I was not the sort of youthful moneyed beauty Sywell was always pursuing.'

She gave a jolly laugh after saying this, and

Marcus could scarcely believe that she was his mother's sister, so unlike was she to her. She took a sip from her glass of Madeira before saying in a more serious voice, 'I think that it is time that I spoke to you about the reason for my asking you to visit me. I have often thought that you ought to be told the truth about your parents' marriage and when I heard from a friend that there had always been some constraint between you and your father, and that they thought it likely that it arose because of their failed marriage, I was more than ever convinced that I had a duty to do so—so here we are.'

She stopped, and now she was so solemn that she was like a different person. 'You must understand that Danielle was a great beauty and it was our parents' hope that she would make a grand marriage. They put a great deal of pressure on her to marry your father, who was known to be the likely Yardley heir, and was then a young man of great promise.

'The trouble was that she had already fallen in love with the heir to the small estate next to ours, and was most reluctant to give him up—except that I think that the notion of becoming Lady Yardley one day attracted her. I regret to say it, but she was always flighty, changed her mind every other day and felt it her duty to attract every young man she met. My parents were eager for her to be married. They thought that it would settle her.

'Alas, once she was married, she became more flighty than ever. She regretted her lost love and made up for it by behaving as wildly as she could without putting herself in danger of society ostracising her. She was very like Lady Caroline Lamb is today: defying all the conventions. The worst thing of all, though, is that her behaviour made your father doubt whether you were truly his son. It was only when, as you reached manhood, your likeness to him became so strong that he could no longer doubt that he was truly your father.'

Marcus gave a great start on hearing this. It explained so much of his father's behaviour to him. He said, and his voice sounded strange to him when he spoke, 'Had he any real reason to believe that she was telling the truth?'

His aunt smiled sadly. 'A little, perhaps, but the pity of it was that Danielle, when they quarrelled, which was often, frequently taunted him with the possibility that he was not your father. It grieves me to say this, but the main reason for the failure of their marriage lay at Danielle's door rather than his. He was, in fact, extremely patient with her. Unfortunately her behaviour resulted in the coolness which lies between you and your father. She was unhappy, made him unhappy and destroyed the affection which should lie between father and son. In all fairness to him—and to you—I thought that you ought to know the truth.

'I understand that his second marriage is a happy one, and that you are fond of your stepmother and she of you—but my poor sister had much to answer for before she died. She had already broken off all ties with our parents and with me—to our great grief.'

Marcus sighed. He thought bitterly of the many years during which he and his father had been estranged. Of late they had come together a little, and now it seemed, if his aunt could be believed—and he thought that she could—that he might be able to heal the breach which misunderstanding had created.

His aunt could see his distress. She said, her voice anxious, 'I hope that I was not wrong to tell you this, but I owed you the truth.'

Marcus leaned forward and kissed her impulsively on the cheek. 'You were not wrong, but right, and I wish that I had known of this before. It must have hurt you to speak so plainly of a sister whom you must once have loved.'

'Yes, you are like your father,' said his aunt. 'Brave and strong-minded. He never once complained to anyone about Danielle's folly, but bore it like a man. He has his reward in Marissa—and, I am sure in you. Now let us talk of other, happier, things. I hope that you will all come to visit me. I should dearly like to see your half-sister and brothers.'

'So you shall,' said Marcus energetically, 'and you shall come to Sophia's wedding, too. After all, you are my aunt and now I owe you a debt of gratitude for telling me the truth.'

All the way home his thoughts ran round and

round his head like animals exercising themselves in a cage. As a child he had always thought that there must be something wrong with him that his father had shown him so little affection. Later, his father's manner had changed a little, and the story his aunt had told him explained why it had. He must try to forget his own resentment and make up for the lost years which lay between them.

Had she seen the last of him? Louise rather doubted it. There was a determination about Marcus Angmering which she found admirable, but which frightened her a little. He had spoken the truth when he had said that there were few places where they might meet, but she had no doubt that one way or another he would contrive to meet her.

She owned a little house in Chelsea to which she retired at the weekend. During the week she lived over the workrooms. She drove her girls hard, but only on five days a week, something almost unknown in the trade, but she had found that they worked better in those five days than those did whose employers demanded longer hours and less kind conditions. She remembered her own harsh youth too well to subject others to it, and it amused her to discover the monetary benefits of a more liberal regime.

Two days after Marcus had visited her she became aware—or thought that she did—that she was being watched. Living with Sywell had given her a sixth sense. Twice she saw the same stranger on the corner when she went out for a stroll in the late afternoon. And could it be simple coincidence that the same stranger appeared on the pavement in front of her Chelsea hideaway, whose address no one, not even her forewoman, knew? They all thought that she lived permanently above the salon.

Had Marcus Angmering had the gall to pay a spy to follow her? She would not put it past him. What could be wrong with her that all the men in her life turned out to be domineering creatures determined to have their own way? Wasn't it enough for her to have had Sywell to endure without another such creature turning up to chase after her?

Or was she seeing enemies around every street corner simply because her past life had made her wary of everyone and everything? She liked to think that, but she could not be sure.

Louise was not mistaken. Marcus had driven straight to the address of the ex-Runner whom he knew his friend Nick Cameron had used to discover what he could about Athene Filmer.

'It's a simple task,' he told the man, whose shrewd face and knowing eyes quickly summed up Marcus as the hard sort of gent who knew what was what—and what he wanted. 'Just find out whether she lives above the shop—or whether she has another home away from it, that's all. And whom she mixes with—if she mixes with anyone, that is,'

Marcus added, remembering that Louise had told him that she didn't move in any circles.

Jackson knew better than to ask m'lord why he wanted to know. He nodded, and promised absolute discretion. 'You may be sure, m'lord, that the job will be done in such a way that she won't know that it's being done at all.'

'Excellent,' said Marcus.

The Earl saw Jackson on his way out. He said, his brows raised a little, 'You have had occasion to employ an ex-Runner, Marcus? They are not always either honest or reliable, but I believe that that man is.'

He did not tell Marcus that Jackson had visited him on behalf of the Home Office over the matter of Sywell's murder, nor did he ask Marcus why he had employed him.

Marcus said quietly, 'My friend Cameron recommended him; he found him honest. I need a confidential matter settled before I leave London.'

The Earl did not ask what the confidential matter was, but began to move away. Marcus said, 'sir, there is something which I wish to say to you and now seems as good a time as any—if you have a moment for me, that is.'

His father turned towards him and said a little heavily, 'I always have time for you these days, Angmering. It is my deepest regret that once I had not. I promise to listen to you and give you my full attention.'

Marcus blinked; it was almost as though his father knew what he was about to say. They moved back into the study. His father did not sit behind his desk, but walked across to sit in a chair by the window. He motioned Marcus to the one opposite.

Now that the moment had come, Marcus found that he was lost for words. Once, when he was younger and rasher, he might have attacked his father with the knowledge of what his aunt had told him, reproached him a little for mistreating him because of what he had thought his mother had done. Now he could only feel pity for a man who had been as much a victim as himself.

'Sir,' he began, 'I met my aunt, my mother's sister, yesterday at her request, not mine. She told me the true story of your marriage, and explained to me why, when I was a child, there was always a strong reserve in your manner to me.'

It was the kindest way he could think of to describe the coldness and lack of interest which his father had shown in him during his childhood. Since the Earl made no immediate answer to him, he ploughed on, finding in himself a diplomacy which he had not known he possessed.

'She also explained why, when I grew up, your manner to me softened a little, and when I look at the portrait of you painted when you were my age now and I look at myself, the strong resemblance between us convinces me, as it must have convinced you, that I am truly your son.'

The expression of pain on his father's face was momentary, but it was there. Marcus felt it incumbent on him to continue. 'My aunt also told me that the fault in your marriage did not lie with you, and that you had shown great patience with my mother's behaviour until the day she passed out of our lives.'

He was silent—and so was his father.

Finally the Earl spoke. 'If I find it difficult for me to answer you, it is because I feel, and have long since felt, shame that I treated an innocent child as harshly as I did. Even if your mother had spoken the truth about your fatherhood I should not have visited her sin upon the head of someone as defenceless as you were then. The constraint which still exists between us comes on my side from my stupidity in allowing a lie to dominate my—and your—life for so long.

'I ask your pardon, and trust that from now on we might become friends. We cannot call back the past and change it, but we can refuse to allow it to poison our lives on the future. My own relief is that my behaviour to you did not harm you—you have turned into the kind of son a father can be proud of. I therefore ask you to forgive me, if you can.'

Marcus leaned forward and said in his straightforward way, 'No forgiveness is needed, sir. Understanding rather, for what my aunt told me made me feel pity for you—and lessened the pity I felt for myself.'

His father rose and put out his hand, saying, 'Let

that serve as an epitaph for the dead past, Angmering, and we will shake on it, if you would. It is fitting that before your sister marries we should come together thus and be able to join in the celebrations as a true father and son at last.'

Marcus rose, too. They stood face to face, the stern father, and the son whose likeness to that father was written on his face, in his voice and in his manner.

'Indeed, sir—and that will be the end of that, I trust.'

His father nodded and they remained silent for a moment, the loud ticking of the clock being the only sound in the room: a fit commentary on the passing of life and time.

Marcus did not have long to wait for his hiring of Jackson to bear fruit; after all—as the man had told him—it was a simple enough task compared with most he was given.

On the following Monday afternoon he arrived in Berkeley Square.

'I think I've found what you want, m'lord. The lady lives over her workrooms in Bond Street during the week. After six o'clock on a Friday she hires a Hackney cab and is driven to a little house in Chelsea not far from the river, where she spends Saturday and Sunday. Sunday she goes to church all respectable like and speaks to no one—other than to shake hands with the Reverend at the end of the service.

'Early on a Monday morning she returns to the shop. She has a couple of servants at her weekend place: a housekeeper and a maid of all work. It seems that she does not mix with her neighbours and during a careful watch she had no visitors other than a lad who delivers milk.'

He paused. 'I have to say that I think she's something of a fly lady, because I suspicioned that she knew that she was being watched. On my first day I perhaps wasn't too careful, since after that every time that she went out she looked around her most busily. I made a few discreet enquiries about her, thinking that they might be useful to you. It seems that she has no gentleman callers, either in Bond Street or in Chelsea. The opinion is that she is lady-like and discreet.'

'Excellent,' said Marcus. 'That is all I need to know. Would you prefer to be paid now?'

'If it suits you, m'lord, yes.'

Feeling a bit of a cur for having Madame Félice watched, Marcus handed him his money on the spot, but he did not feel so much of a cur that he did not glumly regret that he would have to wait until the weekend before he paid her a call!

Saturday morning found him hiring a cab and setting off for Chelsea. Either being a *modiste* paid well, or Madame had a fund of money of her own, for the little house was a jewel of a place, newly appointed and painted. He thought that, apart from the paint, it resembled Madame herself. Whistling gently, he paid off the cabbie and knocked on her elegant front door…

Louise had just finished eating a late breakfast and was drinking a cup of excellent coffee—she always shopped at Jackson's in Piccadilly—when she heard the door knocker and wondered who it could be at this hour.

She did not have long to wait. The little maid came in saying, 'There's a gentleman to see you, mam.'

'A gentleman, Jessie? Did he give his name?'

'No, mam. He said that he thought that you might know who it was? He said that he was in need of a shirt—but, mam, could he really mean that? He was wearing a very fine one.'

'Did he, indeed?' Louise jumped to her feet half-amused, half-scandalised. 'Tell him to go away, at once.'

'Yes, mam.'

Jessie disappeared, only to reappear again a few moments later. 'Oh, mam, he says as how he won't. He says that it's most urgent that he see you, and that he's prepared to wait outside until you're ready to speak to him—and he gave me half a sovereign to tell you that—look!'

Louise, who had sat down, jumped up again. Bribery and corruption of her servant, was it now?

What next would the man get up to? For she had no doubt that it was his lordship of Angmering who had somehow tracked her down.

'Do you want me to give it back to him, mam?' asked her maid anxiously.

'Certainly not, by his behaviour he deserves to lose more than half a sovereign. Tell him that—' Inspiration failed her. Oh, bother the man, what message could she send that would be sure to get rid of him?

'Tell him that if he doesn't go away I shall send for the local constable to remove him,' she came out with at last.

'He won't like that, mam,' said her maid, still anxious.

'I'm sure that he won't, but tell him so all the same.'

Out shot the maid again. Louise picked up her cup and began to drink coffee agitatedly.

This time, though, when the maid reappeared she was trailing in the wake of that haughty aristocrat Marcus Angmering, who was apparently so determined to see her that he would play any trick which his inventive mind could think up.

'I wouldn't wish you to go the trouble of setting the law on me,' he said cheerfully, once the maid had left, 'So I decided to speak to you in person, so that we could settle our difficulties without delay— and pray do not reprimand your maid for letting me in. She found it difficult to deny someone so much larger and stronger than she is.'

Louise stared at him, the coffee cup halfway to her mouth, and to her horror found herself saying, 'What difficulties, sir?' instead of telling him to remove himself from her dining room.

'The difficulties relating to your inability to accept my kind offer of protection.'

She put down her coffee cup with a trembling hand. 'Your impudence, sir, is beyond belief. You force your way into my home, terrorise my servant…'

Marcus interrupted her. 'Oh, scarcely that,' he murmured, his mouth twitching. 'I wouldn't describe giving her half a sovereign as terrorising her.'

'Oh…' Louise gave what could only be called a gasp of exasperation. 'You are no gentleman, sir, you twist every word I say. You know perfectly well what I mean—and there *are* no difficulties about your offer of protection—I refused it in the plainest terms possible.'

'But so quickly,' Marcus protested. 'You didn't even pretend to consider it—which is not the proper way to refuse a business proposition.'

'I never pretend, sir,' and oh, dear what a lie that was, since her whole life, and even her name, was a pretence. 'You have had my answer. Pray allow Jessie to escort you to the door.'

'Without even the offer of a cup of coffee,' he said sadly. 'That's no way to treat a guest, madame.'

'You are not my guest,' she flashed back at him. 'You come here uninvited, force your way in—'

'True,' he said, still sad. 'But how else may I speak with you, tell me that?'

His smile was so wicked, his eyes mocked at her so gently, that Louise felt as though she had begun to melt internally. She had never experienced such a sensation before. No, he was not handsome, but he was better than that—he must be to have such an effect on her. She licked her lips, and saw his expression change when she did so—and wondered why.

Louise was inexperienced in the arts of love because she had never been subjected to anything other than the acts of frustrated lust. She had no notion of what might attract or rouse a man. Marcus, watching her, was, to his surprise, sure that she was truly innocent, and that the signs of fear which she occasionally showed were genuine.

He was suddenly ashamed. He had been teasing her after the fashion in which he teased Sophia and the Two Neds, but where that had been innocent and playful this could be construed as malicious. More so when he could see her quivering lip and her trembling hand.

'I am sorry,' he said. 'I should not be doing this, I did not mean to frighten you. I ought to go.' And he began to turn away from her, to leave by the door by which the little maid had earlier left.

He was going! She would be alone again. Fearful

though she was, Louise found that she did not want that. Beyond the fear of him which Marcus had briefly seen lay something else.

She was so lonely. All her life she had been alone. The only bright stars in it had been her guardian and later Athene Filmer and she had lost both of them. If he left her now, to whom would she speak this day? To the housekeeper, the little maid and later, perhaps, tradesmen, shop-girls, and barely them.

'No,' she said, the words almost wrenched from her, 'don't go. You…I…standing there you tower over me—pray sit down.'

Now what had caused that, Marcus wondered? There was even the faintest hint of a smile on her face, a tremulous one. Was he seeing the first breach in her defensive wall?

He said, as lightly as he could, 'Oh, I am not so tall that I could be called a tower, but you are such a dear little thing that I can see I might appear to be if not a tower, a turret.' And he pulled out a chair and sat opposite to her at table.

Yes, he had provoked a proper, if rueful, smile by his last remark. Emboldened by it, he asked, rather after the manner of a small boy seeking a favour, 'Would your kindness extend to offering me a cup of what smells like excellent coffee? I was so anxious to meet you again that I skipped breakfast.'

Oh, he was impossible! How in the world had he managed to persuade her into not only allowing him to stay, but also to sit there, smiling, as though his proper place was in this room with her as though they had just risen from bed and were being Darby and Joan together.

What was worse was that she was now getting into the spirit of this disgraceful game he was playing with her. She rose, opened the breakfront cabinet which stood behind her and which contained a fine array of good china, took a cup and saucer from it, and poured him his coffee. She pushed it, the jug of cream and the sugar bowl across the table at him.

'My thanks,' he said, and drank the coffee slowly and appreciatively. He looked at her over the top of the cup, and said, now grave, all his former teasing mode gone, 'You must believe me when I tell you that I am going to these lengths because I need to meet you in order to woo you, and you must know how difficult that is going to be—'

'To woo me?' Louise threw at him again. 'To woo me into accepting a proposal to be your mistress is more commonly known as seduction. Have you no respect for virtue?'

Marcus put down his empty cup. 'We could have a useful debate about what virtue consists of—'

'No, we could not. We both know perfectly well what it is. Your behaviour, sir, is abominable—'

'Unlike the coffee,' he interjected, still grave.

'Oh, yes, you *are* impossible. Since you obviously think of me as fair game, why have I allowed you to remain, why?'

'Because,' he said, fixing her with his eyes, 'I

believe that you are as attracted to me as I am to you—is not that so? Believe me that if I made you my *belle amie* I would treat you with the same love and care as if you were my wife—nay, with more love and care than most of my fellows treat their wives. It is not because of your lesser rank that I do not ask you to marry me, it is because I have no intention of ever marrying. With the exception of one, most marriages seem to me to be shams—and I cannot hope that mine would be different from the common run. Accept my offer, I promise to be faithful to you, and do my best to make you happy.'

What he was saying had the ring of truth in it. For what had her marriage with Sywell been but a ghastly travesty of what marriage ought to be? More, she knew how hollow most marriages were. But, and it was a big but, she had a sense of herself, despite all that she had been compelled to do to save herself, as a woman of honour. If virtue and a desire to be honest were all that were left to her, then she must cling to them.

'I believe you,' she said slowly. 'I deem you to be a man of your word, but it is not enough.'

'There is nothing I could say that would change your mind?'

'I can think of nothing.'

He leaned across the table and took her hand. 'I cannot let you go. I need to meet you again, to try to convince you otherwise—'

She shook her head at him.

'No? Not even to meet you as a friend?' What he said next was wrung from him without warning, spontaneously, he could never previously have imagined himself saying such a thing. 'Félice I am a lonely man, and have been so from childhood. If I promised not to badger you or to follow you—'

'Or to have me followed,' she put in.

Marcus bowed his head. 'Yes, forgive me for that, but I was desperate. If I kept my promise to behave myself, could we meet occasionally? If only to talk.'

'How can I believe that you would not—' she began and then, 'But how could we meet? Either in private or in public?'

'Not in society, that is true, but occasionally I could walk with you, or drive you where we are not known.'

'In secret,' Louise said bitterly, thinking that all her life had been one long secret.

'Not entirely,' he told her. 'If you were willing to be a little devious I could be your cousin who has just discovered your whereabouts after many years.'

'M'lord Angmering's unknown cousin?' queried Louise. Her smile was a strange one.

'By no means. I shall be Mr Marks, and we shall be discreetly friendly—if you will permit, that is. Mr Marks's means will be modest—as well as his style.'

Louise gained the distinct impression that M'lord was enjoying himself. He reminded her of a small boy who had been given a new toy. The fear she had felt for him ebbed away a little.

'I should not be listening to you,' she said. 'But—' and she hesitated.

'But you are,' he returned eagerly. 'Think with what pleasure we can meet—simply to converse, of course.'

'Of course,' said Louise her tone sardonic. 'So long as you remember that, m'lord, we shall do well together.'

'Mr Marks,' he corrected her. 'I am to be Mr Marks—you will find our adventure easier since you will retain your name.'

'So long as I retain my honour,' she said, but she was smiling while she said it.

'I promise that Mr Marks will behave himself rather better than Lord Angmering has done. Now inform me that Mr Marks will be allowed to take Madame Félice for a short drive this afternoon—not in M'lord's curricle, but in the Hackney cab in which he will call on you at two of the clock. Reassure your little maid that when he next calls he will behave like a perfect gentleman. In the meantime you may pour me another cup of coffee.'

'Alas, it has grown cold, but perhaps, later this afternoon, when we return from our drive, you will take tea with me.'

Marcus rose and bowed. 'M'lord Angmering will take leave of you, Madame Félice, until this afternoon—when Mr Marks will call on you.'

I must be mad, thought Louise, trembling a little from she knew not what, to allow him any rope at all, any chance for him to start his nonsense with me again. Why in the world have I given way?

She was not being honest with herself and she knew it. She had given way because she had, for once, allowed her heart to overrule her head. She had done so, however, fully aware of the most supreme irony of all: that Marcus Angmering should pretend to be her cousin when he was, in truth, her cousin—even if only a distant one!

Louise was hugging this delightful thought to herself when she walked into the kitchen where the housekeeper and the little maid were in urgent conversation—about her strange visitor, no doubt. She really had no need to explain herself, but thought that it might be politic to do so if Marcus was going to come a-visiting.

'It turns out,' she said after some discussion of what her dinner might consist of, 'that the gentleman who visited me today is my long-lost cousin.' And that was no lie, was it? 'Mr Marks, who has had the good fortune to discover my whereabouts. He will doubtless be calling again.'

If the two women facing her thought that this was the biggest Banbury tale they had ever heard, they offered her no outward and visible sign of their disbelief.

'So that is why he gave me a half-sovereign!' exclaimed the little maid.

'Probably,' said Louise, gratified that she had extricated herself from yet another difficult situation—and hoping that she would not have to do so again… Up to now her life had seemed to consist of one difficult situation after another, and today's was only the latest. She had to hope that her luck, which had held good so far, would not suddenly desert her.

Chapter Three

Marcus Angmering was thinking that luck was with him. Madame Félice's sudden decision to allow him to visit her was promising, to say the least. There was a determination about her, though, which warned him that she would not lightly surrender to his advances. She had received his first overtures with disdain, even though it was plain that she had been attracted to him.

He arrived back at Berkeley Square after his drive with her where he had behaved himself perfectly, to discover that his father had had an unexpected visitor. It was Jackson, whom he met on the point of leaving the house.

'You were looking for me?' he asked a little puzzled.

'Not exactly,' Jackson said. 'I came to see your father in order to clear up some points relating to the Marquis of Sywell's murder. Now that I have seen you, however, I would be grateful if you would agree to speak to me about it.'

Marcus raised his eyebrows. 'Seeing that I was in Northumberland at the time of his murder, I scarcely imagine that I can have anything to tell you which you would find of the slightest use.'

'Nevertheless,' Jackson persisted, 'it is possible that you are aware of something which means little to you, but which would assist me.'

'In that case,' said Marcus, 'go ahead, although I warn you that you might be wasting your time.'

'Oh, I'm willing to risk that,' Jackson said cheerfully as Marcus ushered him into the drawing-room.

'Now, m'lord,' he began. 'I understand that at times you visited Jaffrey House when the Marquis was living at Steepwood. Did you ever meet him, and more importantly, did you ever, by chance, meet, or have occasion to see, his wife?'

Marcus shook his head. 'I was warned by my father to avoid him as much as possible. True, on the very few occasions on which I visited Jaffrey House I occasionally saw Sywell at a distance. Of his life at Steepwood I knew nothing, except for those rumours of which I am sure you have heard.'

Jackson nodded his head thoughtfully. 'As I expected. But his wife, the young Marchioness, did you ever see her? Have you any notion of what she looked like? The thing is, what I find very strange is that no one confesses to having seen much of her at all. If you could remember anything of which you might have heard of—or seen yourself—it would help me.'

Marcus shook his head again. He could hardly tell Jackson that he hated his rare visits to his father and had kept himself to himself as much as possible on them. He thought that might be the end of the interview but Jackson had yet another question for him.

'I understood from one person to whom I spoke that the Marchioness was reputed to be a great friend of Miss Athene Filmer who married an acquaintance of yours. Miss Filmer has given us a description of her which might fit anyone. Now Miss Filmer appears to have had few friends, and I wondered whether you ever saw her with the Marchioness, either when they were children together—or later.'

'I can't exactly remember,' said Marcus, cudgelling his brains. He tried to recall walking in the woods at Steepwood on his visits there. Something fluttered at the edge of his memory. Yes, when he was only a lad of fourteen he had stayed at Jaffrey House for a brief time, and once, when he had been out walking he had come across a young girl who might have been Athene Filmer. She had had another, smaller, girl with her who had tripped while larking around a pond and had cut her knee.

He had stopped and used his handkerchief to clean and bandage the knee and...she had limped off...the flash of memory ended. Except that there had been something about the child which it was important that he should recall. But all that he could remember was that she had had a pretty voice, and so he told Jackson.

'Fairish hair,' he said slowly. 'It was years ago, well before I went to university, that I saw Athene Filmer in the woods at Steepwood with another little girl who had fairish hair, and striking eyes. I suppose that it's possible that she might have been the child who later became the Marchioness. Miss Filmer did say once that she had known her briefly in youth. I can say, however, that I never saw anyone who might be the Marchioness after her marriage to Sywell, because at that time I rarely visited Steepwood.'

What was it about the child's eyes? And what else had briefly intrigued him? He still couldn't remember—it remained on the edge of his mind.

Jackson nodded. 'Fits,' he said briefly. 'I was told that by several who thought that they might have seen her, but that describes too many young women, don't it? It's not particular in any way. And Miss Filmer you said. It's true she hadn't many friends, but one of them is that woman in Bond Street who makes the Quality's dresses.'

'Madame Félice!' exclaimed Marcus. 'She's Athene's friend! How did she come to know her?'

'Exactly,' said Jackson. 'She, the Filmer woman, I suppose that I ought to call her Cameron now, claims that she knows nothing of where the

Marchioness might be—not that I'm after believing her. She's a fly young woman.'

'True,' said Marcus, smiling. 'But it's a big jump from that to suppose that she knows where Sywell's missing wife went when she disappeared.' All the same he was intrigued, and wondered what Jackson would come out with next.

What the man did was to change tack disconcertingly—a favourite trick of his.

'Of course, you know all about your Pa's feud with Sywell, I suppose.'

'Everyone who met him feuded with Sywell,' said Marcus dryly.

'So I'm told. But the more I learn about him the more I learn about the Yardley connection with him. That duel all those years ago, the one where Sywell shot and killed the then Earl—a rum do, that. Burneck's evidence proved that it was a put-up job. Sywell murdered your distant relative and got Steepwood Abbey through it in consequence—not your Pa. It was lost to the Yardleys, apparently permanently.'

Ah, so Jackson was suggesting a motive for his father murdering Sywell, was he? That since Burneck's evidence of Sywell's villainy came *after* Sywell's death, his father might have disposed of him in an effort to regain the Abbey.

'Now, that cock won't fight,' said Marcus coldly. 'The Abbey is worth very little—quite the contrary. Now that my father has recovered it, as a consequence of the fact that Burneck revealed that Sywell gained it fraudulently and murdered my cousin into the bargain, it's going to take thousands to restore. No one but a fool would have murdered the man simply to get it back again.'

'Aye, and your pa ain't a fool,' agreed Jackson. 'I'll grant you that. A pity we have to run anyone in for topping such a regular out-and-outer as Sywell was—but justice must be done, you know. We can't have people running around killing Marquises and getting away with it.'

'Agreed,' smiled Marcus, 'to your first proposition, but not the second—seeing that the law couldn't top Sywell we should be grateful to the man who did. Gave us all a bad name, didn't he?'

Jackson nodded. 'You might say that. Thank you for your time, m'lord—most helpful.' He turned for the door.

'Think nothing of it,' said Marcus to his back as cheerfully as he could, but happy to see him go. He was a little premature, for Jackson swung round as he pushed the door open, and said, 'Oh, and by the by, if you can remember anything more about what Miss Filmer's friend—who might have been Sywell's lady—looked like, pass the news on to me if you would. You know where to find me. I'd dearly like to question her, so I would.'

Marcus stared at the closed door. Now, what was all that about? And Madame Félice, how did she arrive in the conversation? What's her connection with the Steepwood mystery—other than that she was Athene Filmer's friend? And that was something Jackson didn't see fit to tell me when I engaged him to investigate her.

The clever devil obviously guessed that I knew more about Athene's little friend than I could remember, but for the life of me I cannot recall what so intrigued me all those years ago.

Marcus would not have been surprised to learn that Jackson visited Madame Félice on Monday morning, calling at her salon and telling the girl on the shop counter that he wished to see the Missis. In fact Louise told him so when he called at her Chelsea home early on the following Saturday.

She allowed the little maid to let him in, but fixed him with the most freezing stare when he walked into her pretty drawing-room.

'Well, well, Mr Marks,' she said coldly. 'Did you set that man on me, *again?* Because if you did I shall require yet another apology from you.'

'What man?' asked Marcus deviously, knowing perfectly well to whom she was referring.

'Jackson, and don't pretend that you don't know whereof I speak. I saw him watching this house before you had me followed here, and when he arrived, asking to speak to me about my friendship with Athene, I immediately recognised him. He said that although he was an ex-Bow Street Runner he was engaged in government business and because I was

Athene's friend he needed to ask me about her other friends—in particular the missing Marchioness. He mentioned, in passing, but I am sure that it was deliberate, that he had been speaking to you. Did *you* suggest that he came to me? Because if so, you may leave at once.'

'Word of honour,' said Marcus solemnly, putting up his hand. 'I did engage him to find out where you lived, but I said nothing which might send him here to question you. He asked me if I had ever seen the Marchioness, either when she was a child, or later after she had married Sywell, and I told him that I had not.'

'Can I believe you?' Félice's agitation was plain to see. 'If you didn't, why did he visit me?'

'Because he's questioning everyone who had anything to do with Steepwood and Sywell. He even hinted to me that my father had a good motive for killing him—so you are not the only person on his list of those he wishes to interview.'

No, thought Louise, but I am the only one who is the missing Marchioness! The thought made her shiver.

'Can I believe you?'

Marcus went down on his knees beside her chair, and gently took her hands in his.

'Félice, believe me. It was bad enough for me to face his questioning: he made me feel as guilty as any villain in the Old Bailey dock and I certainly would not have had you subjected to him. He reminds me of one of those dogs who gets the bear they are baiting by the throat and won't let go. I promise you that if I ever have you investigated again, I shall ask your permission before I do so! Will that satisfy you?'

She wanted to believe him. He was so blunt and straightforward—even his naughtinesses when he had been teasing her in the shop about making him a shirt, and again when he had visited her for the first time, were mild in comparison with what she knew of the behaviour of other aristocrats who pursued those below them in rank. If he touched her, it was gently—and so far he had rarely done even that.

'So it was his decision that he came to see me? And his only?'

'Yes, I did not send him. If he comes again, be careful—behind that jovial exterior he is clever in the extreme.'

'So I thought—fortunately I had nothing of importance to tell him.' Oh, what a lie that was! Another! For she certainly had no intention of giving her true identity away to Jackson, of all people.

Marcus smiled. 'That would not please him, I think. He is a thief-taker and criminal-catcher, *par excellence*. He resents not being able to track Sywell's murderer down—even though he might think that Sywell deserved to be murdered. His problem is that so many might have wanted to murder him—including his wife.'

'Let us speak of something different. Shall I ring for coffee?'

'I am forgiven, then?'

'Yes, if you like. I don't think that there was anything to forgive, though.'

'And since it is a fine day, even if it is cold, you will walk down to the river with me and watch it flow by.'

All the same, despite the pleasure of being with her there was the agony of not being able to touch her, for the more he was with Félice as he was now beginning to call her, the more his desire for her grew. Not only because of her pretty face and figure, but because he could talk to her as he had never been able to talk to a woman before.

For all her romantic appearance, she was as delightfully down to earth as he was, and did not hesitate to check and challenge him if she disagreed with him. Her pleasures were simple ones, like his.

There was a man with a barrow selling roast chestnuts on the road by the river. Marcus saw her looking wistfully at them and said, waving what Louise always thought of as his lordly hand, 'You would like some?'

'Only if you joined me,' she shot back, 'which would be an odd thing for m'lord to do, would it not? Eat chestnuts in the street!'

'You forget,' he said. 'I am Mr Marks today, and Mr Marks is allowed to be one of the crowd. He is accompanied by no flunkeys, and has no grand position to keep up, something which pleases him. I do not like consequence, my dear Félice, but I am doomed to endure it. Today I am one among many.'

Louise was silent for a moment before she said, 'I think that you truly mean that, Mr Marks. Do you avoid it when you live on your father's estate in the north?' For he had told her that he rarely visited London and preferred the country.

'As much as possible, but *noblesse* does *oblige,* you know, however little I may wish it. It is my duty, you understand.'

'Sywell never thought that,' exclaimed Louise, without thinking.

'No, I believe not, but he was hardly a man one would take as a model of what a man, never mind a nobleman, ought to be.'

When they reached the Embankment they sat on one of the benches which faced on to the river and enjoyed their chestnuts, warming their hands while they ate them from the paper in which the barrow-boy had placed them.

'Chelsea has many places of interest,' Marcus said, 'including the Royal Hospital for the Pensioners. I understand that one may walk in the grounds. There is little to see at this time of the year—other than the building itself, of course. It rebukes me a little, you know, for it is filled with soldiers who have given everything for their country, while I have given nothing.'

He said this with such feeling that, again without thinking, Louise placed her gloved hand on his.

'Should you like to have been a soldier?' she asked him.

'Yes, but my father would not permit it. And even though, in those days, we were at odds, I did not feel that I ought to disobey him. I may even have thought that I might please him by agreeing with him, but…' and Marcus shrugged his shoulders.

He was telling her things which he had never told anyone. Short though their acquaintance was, again, sitting by her, he felt more like Darby and Joan than many a couple who had spent years living together did.

'I suppose I ought not to ask you this, but are you still at odds with him?'

'No, we have become reconciled recently, and I think it is a great relief for both of us. Oh, I always respected him, but I could not love him. That, oddly enough, was reserved for my stepmother and her sons and the daughter whose trousseau you are making.'

He laughed a little, and said, 'I was very happy to gain twin brothers. You have met the Two Neds. I must confess that it was I who nicknamed them.'

He must trust her, thought Louise, a little awed, and also a little ashamed because she felt that she could still not totally trust him, to tell her such things about his family life.

'I like that,' she said, smiling up at him, so that

his heart gave a great leap in his chest, so sweet was her expression. 'Do they like their nicknames?'

'Oh, yes. You see they love to tease me for being old and passé, so I tease them back about being young and flighty—not too severely, mind.'

'How fortunate you are,' she could not help exclaiming, 'to have a loving family. It is something which I have always lacked.'

Her face was so sad when she said this, that Marcus wanted to take her in his arms and kiss and comfort her, while saying: You can always have me for a family, but he had made her a promise to do no such thing, so he merely pressed the hand she had absent-mindedly placed on his, instead.

It grew steadily colder. Marcus offered her his arm and they walked slowly back to her home, where she invited him in to drink tea with her: it had become something of a ritual. On the way they were so engrossed in one another that neither of them noticed a curious pair of eyes watching them. Their owner shook his head, but did not follow them.

All the same when next he met Angmering he meant to twit him about what must be his newest conquest: it was the little *modiste,* no less, who had successfully held off every man who had made so much as a bow in her direction. Sandiman was not the only unfortunate who had felt the rough edge of her tongue. One wondered what spell Angmering had cast on her that she could look so trustingly up at him.

Marcus had, as he had promised, behaved himself on their little excursion, though, God knows, he had been hard put to do so! He was equally well-behaved as he drank tea and talked about the clown, Grimaldi, who like Madame Félice he had seen performing at Sadler's Wells.

She was too young, she said, to have been taken to see the precocious Master Betty, who had entertained London for a short time nearly eight years ago, before the notion of seeing a young boy impersonate Shakespearian heroes had palled.

'So,' Marcus exclaimed, 'we have another common love: the theatre. If it were not that we might be seen I should be happy to escort you there one evening. It's a pity we don't live in the middle of the last century when you could have worn a mask without comment—but as it is...' and he grimaced.

Louise thought it a pity, too, but did not say so; she felt it best not to offer Marcus too much of herself. The more she was with him, the more she liked him—she dare not use the word love any more than Marcus did, for to do so might launch them into unknown territory.

'And I may come again next week?' he asked her before he left for home, having taken her hand and kissed the back of it, an apparently innocent action which had both parties asking themselves before they parted what it was about the other which affected them so strongly.

Louise asked herself the most questions about this. She was not so knowing as Marcus was. No man had ever roused her, and her late husband had treated her so roughly that she had no notion of the profound influence which the presence of a member of the opposite sex could have upon her body. Other than revulsion, that was, she had experienced a great deal of that!

Now with Marcus all was different. The day seemed to brighten when she was with him; for him to touch her, even lightly, was to awaken strange sensations whose origin was a mystery to her.

No novel she had ever read had spoken of such things. All was decorous. Men and women might banter with one another, but these other stirrings which were affecting her so strongly were never mentioned. For the first time she could understand why women could be seduced by love, for not only the man, but their body also, was betraying them.

So even though she said, 'Yes, indeed,' to his wish to visit her on the next Saturday, she told herself firmly, once the door shut behind him, to be sure to go carefully with him, for the biggest traitor in her camp of virtue was none other than herself!

Marcus found himself at something of a loose end. Back at his country home there was always something for him to do, some problem to solve, some decision to make, some friends to visit or go riding with.

Here in London, though, the days passed in unchanging idleness. He could see why many of his contemporaries drank, gambled and wenched so much—they had little else to do. There was a limit to the length of time that he could sit and read a book, however improving. If he were compelled to live here permanently, he told himself that he would find something interesting to pursue—set up a laboratory, experiment with velocipedes, or study in detail the theory of scientific farming.

Or he might go in for being a diplomat, like Lord Granville Leveson Gower, which was a bit of a joke seeing how undiplomatic he usually was! Or become an MP. Anything would be better than doing nothing. As it was, since he would shortly be returning to the north where he was both happy and useful, he hadn't the time to start anything new.

Wednesday morning thus saw him decide to visit Gentleman Jackson's gymnasium at 13 Bond Street. This also had the advantage of not being far from Madame Félice's work rooms, which gave him the added bonus of perhaps catching a glimpse of her. He could scarcely wait for the weekend to come round again when he might be with her—but he had given his word of honour not to badger her, so he must try to distract himself with other activities, preferably physical ones.

Jackson's was crowded when he reached there.

Among the men present, some already changed to spar with one of his bruisers, were Sharnbrook, his sister's future husband, and Jack Perceval. Jack was busy towelling himself off. He waved at Marcus when he saw him, and mouthed something incomprehensible in his direction.

Marcus shrugged and sat down, and waited for the Gentleman, who was busy, to attend on him. Jackson was something of a friend, for he respected Marcus's straightforward approach to life, as well as his good left hook. He was not one of those who played at being a bruiser—he worked at it on the few occasions he was in London.

This sitting about, though, left him a target for Jack, who accosted him cheerfully while Marcus was talking to Sharnbrook.

'You're a downy bird, Angmering, and no mistake! How the devil did you get that haughty piece to eat out of your hand while the rest of us were trying to persuade her to look in our direction, not arm in arm it with her down the King's Road and the Embankment?'

Marcus gave Jack a look which ought to have slain him at ten paces, but didn't.

'Don't know what you mean, old fellow.'

The words 'old fellow' sounded as though they were a curse, which Marcus meant them to do. It was a wretched nuisance that one of the Ton's greatest gossips should have seen him with Madame

in Chelsea—and what the devil was Jack Perceval
doing there, anyway?

Jack put his finger by his nose. 'Oh, damn that
for a tale, Angmering. Were you, or were you not,
squiring that pretty little filly Madame Félice in
Chelsea last weekend—or have you both acquired
doubles?' He gave a great bellow of laughter as he
ended.

Marcus could feel Sharnbrook's knowing eyes on
him. Since his relationship with Madame was an innocent one he was feeling something strange—that,
for once, he was an aggrieved party. He was also
feeling something else strange, and savage—that he
would like to plant a real facer on Jack Perceval's
inadequate chin to teach him not to take a virtuous
woman's name in vain. Marcus had thought that
Jack had become his friend and would thus have the
decency to keep quiet about what he had seen. On
the other hand, though, he supposed gloomily that
the temptation to pass on such a rare piece of gossip
was too great for him.

Well, he would make sure that Jack would keep
silent, for the thought of the knowing laughter and
the hilarity about Madame's supposed fall from
grace was too much for him to contemplate.

So, he rose, leaned forward, took hold of the
towel which was now round Jack's neck, and using
both his hands, tightened it gently, while saying,
'What do I have to do, Perceval, to stop you from
jeering in public about a woman who has never be-

haved in such a manner that you have the right to doubt her virtue—and mine—come to that? What would it take, Perceval?' and he tightened the towel a little further as though he intended to use it as a garrotte.

He had no notion of how savage he looked when coming out with this. His face white, Jack spluttered, 'Come off it, Angmering, I didn't mean anything you know—only the give and take we all go in for, you must know that.'

'No, I don't know it, Perceval, and I'll thank you not to blow smoke on any woman's good name when I'm present. Just tell me you won't do so again, and I'll not twist your head off its shoulders.'

Sharnbrook put a hand on Marcus's arm. 'Steady on, old fellow. Don't threaten to murder poor Jack because he's a bit of an idiot. We all know that, don't we, Jack?'

'Yes, but does *he* know it?'

'He does now,' grinned Sharnbrook. 'Say pretty please, I'll be a good chap in future, and Angmering will let you go, won't you?' and he tightened his grip on Marcus's arm.

Reluctantly Marcus released the stutteringly apologetic Jack, dropping his hands, just as the Gentleman came over, saying in his quiet way, 'Now gentleman, no brawling, please, reserve that for the ring. As for you, Mr Perceval, you should be aware by now that I have a rule that we don't tattle about the fair sex in here. Remember that in future.'

'I didn't mean anything by it,' grumbled Jack, his head bent.

'In that case, sir, if you didn't, best not to say anything, eh?'

On that the Gentleman left them, leading Sharnbrook away. He said quietly to him while he laced the gloves on to the Duke's hands, 'I never thought m'lord Angmering had such a short fuse. He's always struck me as the easy-going kind.'

'Oh, where women are concerned,' returned Sharnbrook, falling into a fighting pose, 'we've all got short fuses. Depend upon it, Angmering is in a bad way—and for the first time, I would hazard. And now, let's to work.'

Unaware that, for the first time, she had become the public target of unkind gossip, Louise was working on Sophia Cleeve's trousseau. She had cut out the wedding gown herself, and was busy basting the skirt together when the girl in the shop came in to tell her that the Bow Street Runner was back, asking to see her again.

'Again!' exclaimed Louise, almost sticking a pin into her hand rather than the pin-cushion, so shocked was she by Jackson's return. She had thought to see the last of him, and didn't relish yet another session of polite verbal fencing.

On the other hand, to refuse to see him might look too particular.

'Tell him he may interview me in my office at the back. I'll go there immediately.'

She had no wish to see the man in public with her girls' curious eyes on her. When Jackson finally walked in she said frostily, 'I do hope that you have a good reason for coming here again, Mr Jackson. My good name will suffer if it becomes known that I am constantly being questioned by a prominent thief-taker.'

'Sorry about that, madame,' said Jackson, not looking sorry at all. 'But I am trying to tie some loose ends up, that's all. It's about your early days at Steepwood. I think we've established that you didn't meet the Marchioness when she was living there with her husband—or did we? I think you also said that you knew Miss Filmer, I mean Mrs Cameron, when you were girls together. Correct me if I am wrong.'

'You are not wrong,' said Louise, still frosty. 'Is that all that you've come to say? If so, you might have saved yourself the visit.'

Jackson pulled a grubby piece of paper out of his pocket and stared at it, before scratching his head, and muttering, 'Ah, yes, that's it. What I didn't ask you was whether *you* met the Marchioness when she was a little girl—Louise Hanslope by name—when you were also Mrs Cameron's playmate. One might suppose that you did. If so, perhaps you could give me a description of her. You see, it's an odd thing, but few people seem to have seen her, and what they remember ain't much.'

'You're asking me if I remember a little girl whom I must have last seen years ago in the hope that it might help you to trace a grown woman? I find that even odder than people not being able to remember a woman whom they have rarely seen. No, I cannot remember meeting her, never mind remembering what she looked like.'

What was beginning to frighten her was that Jackson was starting to ferret out the connection between little Louise Hanslope, the missing Marchioness and Madame Félice. His next question proved that she was right to be troubled.

'Well, there is another possible connection, madame. You see, I recently learned, quite by accident, you understand, that Louise Hanslope left the district when still almost a child, to be apprenticed to a dressmaker. You being in that line of business yourself, I wondered if you had ever come across her?'

Oh, yes, the man was more than a ferret, he was a bloodhound: a bloodhound who was threatening the safe life she had built for herself.

'May I ask where this child was apprenticed, Mr Jackson?'

He inspected his grubby piece of paper again.

'In Northampton, as I understand.'

'Northampton!' Louise began to laugh, something which she found difficult to control, for hysteria was threatening. 'No, I have never met the lady—my apprenticeship was elsewhere. I'm afraid that I cannot be of any assistance to you.'

Jackson stuffed his piece of paper into his pocket. 'Pity, that. I wouldn't have troubled you, if it weren't that I seem to be coming up against a brick wall where the lady is concerned. You must forgive me for bothering you again, but I have to inspect every avenue which might lead me to her.'

'Oh, yes, I do understand that. Will that be all?'

Jackson did not immediately answer her. He made for the door, but before he laid his hand on the knob, he turned and said in an off-hand voice, 'I'm not sure. I hope not to come back to you again, but there is one thing which still puzzles me.'

'Pray what is that, Mr Jackson?' This question was wrung from her, for she did not really want to know the answer since she might not like it. She had become suddenly sure that the man suspected something and was baiting her.

'One of the teachers at Mrs Guarding's school remembered that little Louise was very proficient in French for one so young—that was why I thought that you might—' he paused as though searching for a word, came out triumphantly with '—that you might know her—seeing that you are French yourself. However, seeing that you tell me that you don't, then that cock won't fight, will it? If you'll pardon the expression.'

He still showed no signs of leaving. Louise said, as coolly as she could. 'Will that really be all this time, Mr Jackson? I am a very busy woman, with several trousseaus to complete. So far as I am concerned, gossip about the distant past is an unwanted luxury.'

Jackson's smile for her was that of a tiger contemplating its prey.

'All for today, I think, Madame. Good afternoon to you, I will see myself out.'

Louise sank down into a chair and put her hot face into her hands. He knows! Or he suspects, that I am the Marchioness—but he cannot prove it yet.

When, and if, he can, what then?

Never mind that I can prove that I couldn't have killed my late, unlamented husband, the scandal which would follow such an unmasking would be my ruin.

Chapter Four

'Oh, dear, Madame,' said Cardew, the Yardleys' butler, 'I regret to have to tell you that m'lady and Lady Sophia are not yet ready for you. They send you their apologies, but they had an unexpected visitor this morning, and are at present enjoying a very late nuncheon. They asked if you would kindly agree to wait for them in the picture gallery, where they have sent you coffee and ratafia biscuits. Your footmen and maid are welcome to eat in the kitchen.'

The butler's expression showed what he thought of visitors who were inconsiderate enough to arrive in the morning, and with exquisite courtesy he led Madame to the picture gallery. This was a grand name for a long corridor lined with family portraits and some dated landscape paintings. Sure enough, there was a low table waiting for her with the promised coffee and biscuits on it.

Louise sat down, drank the coffee, which a watching footman considerately poured for her, and nibbled at the biscuits before deciding to pass the time by inspecting the paintings. She gave a cursory glance at the landscapes, which were conventional in the extreme, before she passed on to examine the portraits of past members of the Cleeve family, which included some going back for more than two hundred years. After all, they were her relatives, and it would be nice to know what they looked like, and if she resembled them in any way.

She had just reached a section devoted to some of their wives when the door at the far end opened and Marcus entered. She was so engrossed in inspecting all her unknown ancestors that she did not hear him…

Marcus had spent the morning discussing his future with his father. It was the first fruits of their reconciliation and the two men were easier with each other than they had ever been.

'I want to continue to live at Jaffrey House,' his father had said. 'It is more my home than the Abbey ever was. On the other hand I am determined to restore the Abbey to its former glory, which will mean a fair amount of restoration and rebuilding. Sywell looted it of the little furniture that was left and consequently the interior looks more like a dog kennel than the ancestral home it ought to be.

'My present secretary and librarian tells me that a curse was put on Steepwoods thousands of years ago, by the pagans who created the Sacred Grove and the rune stone. All those who came after them who failed to worship the stone, but followed false Gods, would be doomed to perpetual unhappiness and ruin. Steepwood's chequered history, he said, seemed to bear out the existence of the curse.

'First the Abbey founded here was dissolved and ruined, and every owner of it, all the way down the centuries, lived a tragic life, including Sywell who met with a terrible end. So I am inclined to agree with him that there was such an unlikely thing as a curse, and that it has persisted right down to the present day. Bearing that in mind, I am going to ask you to think carefully about a proposal which I am about to make to you, for that proposal involves the ownership of the Abbey.

'The local landowner who bought much of the Abbey's lands from Sywell has fallen heavily into debt and has asked me to buy them back, to which I have agreed. They will, however, need a great deal of work done with them before they become profitable again. Since you have made such a good fist of restoring the northern estates I am going to ask you to take on the task of doing the same thing for Steepwood's. At the same time you could begin to renovate the Abbey with a view to making it your permanent residence when I am gone to my last rest.

'Jaffrey House could then be the home of the dowager—but such decisions will, of course, be yours to make in the future, not mine. You need not give me an answer immediately, but I would like one soon. Such an ambitious project will have the merit of making work for the local people, and when it is finished will provide permanent employment for the large staff needed to run it.'

Marcus had stared at his father. 'You are sure that you want to do this, father? One might have thought that after waiting so long to regain the Abbey you would wish to begin its restoration yourself.'

His father had shaken his head. 'I am too old, Angmering. I am over seventy and wish to secure the family's future, by giving you *carte blanche* in this matter, since you have proved how responsible you are over and over again. Think of it as reparation for my neglect of you in the past. It is my hope that you will soon marry and settle yourself and your wife at Steepwood as soon as possible. But I also thought that you ought to know of the curse before you make your decision.'

Marcus's immediate response had been to refuse, and then he thought that, after all, his work in Northumbria was done. He could employ a good agent there to run the reformed and rescued lands. Here he had been thinking that he might need occupation and his father was giving him the opportunity of a lifetime—to restore the neglect of centuries, for previous Earls of Yardley had been careless of the land.

As for the curse, he thought nothing of that. He was a true child of the Enlightenment, which had rejected such medieval notions, and possible fear of it would play no part in his decision-making.

His father had again spoken of him taking a wife, and for the first time Marcus did not reject the notion out of hand. A wife would be a great help when the time came to refurnish the Abbey—otherwise he would be entirely in the hands of the furniture makers, bibelot sellers and upholsterers, would he not? He could imagine Félice running round with bolts of cloth, inspecting carpets and mirrors and... His stepmother had told him that her taste was impeccable.

He became aware that his father was expecting some sort of answer from him. He would give him one, and one which he hoped would prove acceptable.

'I cannot say that you have done other than surprise me,' he said at last. 'A month ago I might have given you a different answer. All I can tell you at the moment is that I am inclined to agree to what you wish, but I would like a few days to think it over. You know me, Father. I need to consider a proposition as grand as this carefully, not rush into it without thought.'

'Agreed, Angmering,' said his father. 'But pray do not take too long before you give me your final answer. I am an old man, and I would like to know that I am leaving a sound ship behind me before I finally hand it on to a new captain.'

They had talked of minor matters before his father

left him to visit Whitehall. Marcus made his way downstairs, where he met Cardew in the Entrance Hall. He had always believed that servants knew more about their masters than their masters thought that they did, and Cardew promptly proceeded to prove him right.

'Ah, m'lord, a word with you,' he said. 'M'lady and Lady Sophia have taken their nuncheon late today and have asked the *modiste* who has arrived for a fitting to wait for them in the picture gallery, where I have provided her with coffee and biscuits.'

He paused, looking as though he expected some kind of response.

Marcus said, a trifle impatiently—his mind was full of his recent conversation with his father. 'And, Cardew, and? There must be a point to this.'

'Oh, m'lord, just that I thought that you might like to know that Madame Félice is here.'

'Did you, indeed?' And of course the man was right, but damn everything, how did *he* know that Lord Angmering was greatly taken with the *modiste?* Did the whole world know—and how?

Marcus decided not to try to find out. He said instead, 'Thank you for that useful information, Cardew. Tell me, do you think that Madame might care to make me a shirt?'

He had succeeded in rattling the perfect servant— but not for long. Cardew smiled and said, 'Oh, m'lord, I am sure that you could find that out for yourself,' and walked away, cat-footed.

Well, well, well, why not take the hint and visit Madame—since there were no secrets in the Cleeve household he might as well take this splendid opportunity to be alone with her—quite respectably.

He ran lightly back upstairs, and turned on the first landing towards the door which led to the picture gallery. He pushed it open to see Félice standing about halfway along it, looking up at a portrait of his great-great aunt, Adelaide Cleeve.

She had not heard him arrive, and he remained where he was to study her at leisure. She had her head tipped back and was inspecting the painting with the care with which she did everything. A wall lamp threw a halo of light on her head—and in that moment two things happened.

The first was that he knew that firm little chin—and now he knew where he had seen it before. On a child in the woods at Steepwood who, when he had bandaged her leg, had thrust that same determined chin at him, and had said, 'I am not a coward, boy, even if I am a girl!' A child who had been with Athene Filmer and about whom Jackson had been so recently questioning him.

As if that were not strange enough, the second thing which struck him was bizarre in the extreme. For the living and vibrant woman standing in the corridor and the long dead one whose painted face was hanging on the wall were so alike that they might have been twins.

He could not doubt that Madame Félice was no

Frenchwoman, but was little Louise Hanslope grown up, the Louise Hanslope who had become Sywell's Marchioness—and what would Jackson make of *that?* And what did he, Marcus Cleeve, Lord Angmering, the Earl of Yardley's heir, make of a woman who bore the face and colouring of the Cleeves—and why on earth had he never noticed that before?

He was dumbstruck, until Louise moved and, moving, saw him. He thought that the expression on her face might match that on his own, since it was one of complete and utter disbelief.

They stared at one another. Marcus was the first to move. He said, and his voice sounded hollow in his ears.

'I've seen you before, haven't I? Years ago.'

He had not meant to say any such thing. He was aware that it sounded like an accusation, but he could not help himself, the shock was too great.

Louise genuinely had no notion to what he was referring. All she could think to say was, 'Why? Why do you think that? How could you have seen me?' The expression on his face shocked her. She had wanted to be playful—as she usually was with him, to come out with something like, 'My dear Mr Marks, whatever can you mean?' but the words had stuck in her throat.

Marcus was so surprised that he scarcely knew to which puzzle to address himself. The puzzle of discovering that Madame Félice was almost certainly

Louise Hanslope—and all that that implied—or the other puzzle, that of her likeness to his female ancestor.

'Are you telling me that you do not remember having met me before?' he finally said, aware how inadequate such a lame response was.

'Not to my knowledge,' Louise said. 'Why do you think that we have?'

Something about his expression was beginning to alarm her. The discovery of her likeness to Adelaide Cleeve had not frightened her—but the thought of Marcus's response to it had. His claim that they had met before was a mysterious one, and she needed to know why he had made it. The rapport which had been growing up between them was near to shattering—if it were not shattered already.

'You really do not remember?'

To be fair, he thought, perhaps, she didn't. After all, she must have been very young, and although a young girl might, as she grew older, retain a likeness to the child she had been, a boy was likely to change completely in looks between the age of fourteen and thirty.

'It was at Steepwood,' he said. 'I was out walking and met you there one afternoon when you were still a child. I am not sure how old you were. You were with Athene Filmer, and you tripped and fell, cutting your knee. I used my handkerchief to bind it. I remember I asked you not to cry, and I believe you said something to the effect that you weren't a coward—I can't remember the exact words.'

He saw her face change even as he spoke. Louise's memory of the incident was a faint one, but it was there, waiting to be called into existence by some accident, some trick of fate.

'*You* were that boy? I remember, dimly, something like that happening—but you do not resemble in the least the boy who helped me. I should never have known you, and even now it is only because you have told me of the incident that I can believe it was you. Why are you looking at me like that, m'lord?'

'Mr Marks,' Marcus said, automatically. 'I am Mr Marks to you, remember.'

'Not here,' she said. 'Not now. And something else is troubling you, isn't it?'

'Many things,' he said. 'That you are not French, that, if I am right, you are Louise Hanslope and Sywell's widow, and that you have said nothing to me of this—nor to Jackson, either. Why? Why the secrecy? From what I have heard, and what I know of you, it is most unlikely that any accusation that you murdered Sywell could possibly stand...'

He ran out of breath.

'Well, m'lord,' said Louise, seeing her bittersweet affair with Mr Marks dying before her, 'I'm happy that you are willing to concede that I am no murderess, which I assure you that I am not. But I must say again that something else is troubling you, and I am asking you what that is?'

'You know,' he said—and pointed to the portrait before which they were both now standing. 'It is this—that if you are Louise Hanslope it beggars belief that you have the face of Adelaide Cleeve. How many mysteries are you concealing, Madame Félice—and why?'

'Oh,' Louise said, bitter regret consuming her that he should find out her secrets in this fashion, and furiously aware that he, one day to be the lord of all, who lived out his cushioned life in luxury, should be so ignorant of the hard and difficult lives of the lowly, among whom she had been thrown to live by cruel chance.

'What can such a poor creature as I am do, m'lord, when I face ruin at every turn if my true identity is revealed, but protect myself in the only way I can. If Jackson discovers that I am Louise Hanslope, the missing Marchioness, and makes it known to the world, what price my peace of mind, and the business which I have built up with such care? What would be left to me in order to survive, but to accept your dishonourable offer, and when you grow tired of me, sink down as so many women do, to a short and disgraceful life?'

'No,' said Marcus, trying to take her into his arms. 'Trust me a little—tell me Louise Hanslope's history, and tell me—if you know—why you look like my family, the Cleeves.'

Could she trust him? Must she trust him? It seemed that she had no alternative but to do so. What was she to do for the best?

Louise looked up and saw Mr Marks again. Something she had said had changed him. The look of accusation had left his face, and if she saw only pity there, then that was better than anger, was it not?

'I should speak to you of this, m'lord, and will do so. I will not apologise for what I have done, but I will explain why I have kept my secrets from a harsh world. After that, if you wish you may judge me and leave me, if what I have done disgusts you.

'But we cannot speak of it here, not now. Lady Yardley and Lady Sophia will be with me at any moment, and I have a commission to fulfil. The world's work does not stop because M'lord Angmering needs some answers to his questions. I will take the day off tomorrow—I was thinking of doing so, and Mr Marks may visit me in Chelsea if he will leave Lord Angmering at home.'

Oh, she was a gallant creature, if a devious one, and he would agree to do as she wished, because she was the woman he had hoped to meet and he could not, must not, lose her now.

Louise could not sleep that night. She had managed to go through her dressmaking duties with the Countess and her daughter without betraying the distress which had inevitably followed her unmasking.

She had known that Marcus was clever, but not how clever. Clever enough, once he had recognised her—and that after so many years—to grasp at once who she might be. That it was unlikely—as Jackson must also think—that lonely Athene Filmer had had two young friends, not one, and that that friend must be the lost Marchioness.

The only thing which he had not pursued was why she was so like the Cleeves, and if she were going to tell him the truth about Louise Hanslope and how she came to marry, and then desert, Sywell, she also owed him the duty of telling him the most amazing truth of all—who she really was.

And that would be her biggest problem. The problem which kept her awake that night. For would he believe the truth? Or would he think that she was inventing it to claim a name and a lineage which were not hers. However difficult that might be, though, she must bite the bullet. She could not deceive him further if she were to retain his respect, never mind his love.

She might mock him by calling him Mr Marks, she might hold him off when he wished to make her his mistress, she might deny to him that he meant very much to her, but she could not deny the biggest truth of all: that she loved him.

The kind boy who had bandaged her damaged knee had turned into a strong and kind man—however bluff he was to those around him, his essential goodness shone through. She had no idea of how much Marcus's hard life had made him the sterling man he was, but she knew that man and knew him well.

Despite that she would never be his doxy, his light of love, however much she loved him. For she would be as true to herself as he was to himself, and what would follow from that, only time would tell. Worse than that, who and what she was, and what he would learn of her, might stand in the way of their happiness.

Trust me, he had said, and no one had ever said that to her before.

Consequently, on the following morning, she awaited his arrival in a fever of anticipation. She had thought that he might adhere to the code of conduct which said that the quality did not call in the morning, but, as she ought to have guessed, no such thing. Mr Marks and Marcus, Lord Angmering, made up their own rules.

He had been considerate enough to allow her time to breakfast, but the moment that the French clock on her mantelpiece tinkled out eleven, he was at her door. He was very much Mr Marks, simply dressed, as usual, so as not to attract attention: he might have been a lawyer's clerk, and Louise fleetingly wondered what his valet made of him.

She was not to know that he was his valet's despair. He had once dressed his master in a white satin court suit, and had occasionally kitted him out as a dandy, but was more likely to have to help him into the clothes of a labourer, or a gamekeeper when he was running his father's northern estates.

Louise felt awkward when the little maid showed him in, but she might have guessed that Marcus's manner to her would be unchanged.

His bow was as deep as ever. He accepted the glass of Madeira which she offered him as though this was simply a courtesy call, not a ritual during which Louise would make a full confession to him. He was not yet to know how full and surprising that confession would be, but he would not allow it to change the loving consideration with which he had always treated her until that fatal moment when he had seen her in the picture gallery.

For a moment they sat facing one another, speaking of banalities: the weather, that her session with Sophia and her mother the previous afternoon had been a successful one. Louise thought that Marcus's face was a little shadowed as though he, too, had passed a bad night, but she said nothing of that.

Finally, their conversation ran down. Louise put down her glass, from which she had drunk little, and began, 'M'lord—'

'Mr Marks,' he said. 'Here I am Mr Marks.'

'Very well, Mr Marks. I said that I would tell you the truth about the life of Louise Hanslope whom you have known as Madame Félice, and however much it pains me to relive it, it is my duty to you, and to the truth, to reveal everything. First of all I must tell you that Louise Hanslope is no more my real name than that of Madame Félice Morisot is. If, when I tell you my true name, you wish to leave and to forget that you ever knew me, I shall quite understand. It is a risk which I must take.'

She paused, not knowing how to continue.

Marcus said, gently, 'It is a risk which I must take also. But it is not, I think, a great one.'

'So you say now, not knowing it. When you have heard me out, you may think differently.'

'That's as maybe,' said Marcus gravely. 'But first, tell me your story and allow me to be the best judge of how I react to it.'

'Very well, but before I begin you must understand that some of what I shall be telling you was told to me. John Hanslope was not my father. He was first the bailiff of the Earl of Yardley who lost the Abbey, and then of the Marquis of Sywell who cheated him out of it. Consequently he knew the family well, and in particular Lord Rupert Cleeve, who was, of course, your distant relative. He ought more properly to have been known as Lord Angmering, but for some reason of which I am unaware, preferred not to be.

'It seems that Lord Rupert, to the anger of his father, the Earl, married a French lady, Marie de Ferrers, who was a Catholic. The Earl repudiated him and forbade him the house. He even suggested that since the lady was a Catholic their marriage was not a legal one. Lord Rupert, however, told the bailiff when he left his wife and child—a little girl—

with him, while he looked for a home for them, that the marriage was legal.

'This is the difficult part of my story, for the little girl was none other than myself, Louise Cleeve. I cannot, of course, remember any of this, for I was only a baby then.'

Marcus gave a short exclamation. Louise, her eyes wide and troubled, stopped, but he waved her on.

'John told me later that my father returned and took us away. He later discovered that he left my mother in Cheltenham while he went back to France to recover her inheritance. This was of course, all taking place after the French Revolution had started. My father had quarrelled with my grandfather over that as well. He was at first very sympathetic towards the revolutionaries. Later, when the Terror began he changed his mind. Unfortunately he became trapped in France and died there, exactly how, no one knew.

'So Lord Rupert, my father, never returned from France. John never learned whether he met my mother's family again—or even whether they had also died in the Terror as so many aristocrats did.'

'Which, of course,' interjected Marcus, 'means that if your story is true you are, by rights, the Honourable Miss Louise Cleeve.'

Louise nodded and continued. 'John heard nothing more from Lord Rupert or his wife, although he tried to trace them, until he received a letter from my mother telling him of my father's death in France, and that she was living in great poverty in Cheltenham and was dying. She begged him to help her for the sake of her child, myself. She had not approached the Earl for assistance because she didn't want him to have the care of her Catholic-bred child. She was unaware that he had already died, and that your father, a distant cousin, had inherited the title.

'John immediately drove to Cheltenham and reached us in time to be present at my mother's death.'

Her voice faltered. She swallowed tears, before saying, 'I can just remember her death and John arriving, but only after a jumbled fashion. I have, of course, no memory of my father. Before she died my mother begged John to adopt me, for he too was a Catholic, and also to ensure that, as soon as possible, I took my rightful place in the world. He agreed and took me to Steepwood. Unfortunately my guardian, as John Hanslope became, could find no proof that my father and mother had ever married. He could only assume that they had done so in France, although from something that Lord Rupert had once said to him it seemed that they might have been married in England, after all.

'Lacking proof, the Hanslopes brought me up as their own, since they could find no evidence of my legitimacy and would even have found it difficult to prove that I was an illegitimate child of the Cleeves.

Mrs Hanslope had been a governess in a French family, spoke French well, and taught me the language from infancy. She also gave me an excellent education. I had no notion at this time that I was Louise Cleeve. I assumed that my parents had bequeathed me to my guardian and his wife because my true family was poor. It was only years later that John—my father as I called him then—told me the truth.'

Marcus had said nothing while this remarkable story was unfolded. Louise looked across at him and said, 'It is like a Gothic novel, is it not? Something out of one of Mrs Radcliffe's tales. I can quite understand why my guardian did not wish to subject me to the scandal and unpleasantness of proving my birth when I had no evidence to support it.'

'If this story is true,' murmured Marcus, 'and I can see that you believe it is, I still fail to understand why, when my father returned from India, the Hanslopes did not contact him and inform him of your existence.'

'By the time he returned it was too late. Mrs Hanslope had died, the Marquis of Sywell had taken up permanent residence at the Abbey, and since I had always enjoyed dressmaking John apprenticed me to a French sempstress, an *emigré* who had moved to Northampton where she worked for the nobility and gentry. She thought that I had real talent and wished to recommend me to another French dressmaker in London. Before I could move there,

I returned to the Abbey to visit my guardian who was dying.'

She gave a sad little laugh. 'It seemed that I was doomed to lose everyone I loved. Just before he died I met Lord Sywell. He was not quite the debauched wreck he afterwards became and still possessed some of the charm which I understand was his in youth. He became obsessed with me, and of all things offered me marriage. I refused him at first, but when I told my guardian he urged me to accept him.

'It was then that he first told me that I was Lord Rupert's child but that I had no means of proving that I was a Cleeve or that I was legitimate. He said that by marrying Sywell I could regain my place in society and that if I had a child, the Cleeves would have returned to the Abbey which they had lost. Remember that I was very young and innocent and that I was about to lose the last person in the world who could be called my family. I was shortly to be left quite alone. I shall never know why Sywell did not simply take me by force and make me his mistress—but he was a man of great caprice and perhaps it amused him to marry a bailiff's daughter. By then, of course, no genteel family would have allowed their daughter to marry him.

'So, we were married, and it was the worst thing which I could have done. I will not weary you with the story of my life with him. Suffice it to say that it was one long agony. Fortunately for me I was, from my wedding day, his wife in name only, which did not prevent him from tormenting me in other ways. Only my renewed friendship with Athene Filmer saved my sanity. Finally, one day, I decided to run away to try my fortune in London, as my old mistress had suggested. I shall always wonder why he married me at all.

'I felt no compunction about robbing Sywell of both money and jewellery before I left; he owed me that as compensation for the ill-treatment which I had endured from him. I used it to set up my business, of which you know. That, Lord Angmering, is my story, and whether you consider me to be deluded, an impostor, or even the true descendant of the Cleeves, either legitimate or illegitimate, is your choice to make, since I have no proof to offer that any of my sad tale is true—other than that I am Sywell's widow and John Hanslope's adopted child.'

Silence fell in the pretty little room. Marcus had listened to Louise's sad tale first with interest, mixed up with an element of disbelief, and then with shock when she had spoken so measuredly of her dreadful life with Sywell.

'One thing is sure, though,' he said at last. 'You have the face of the female Cleeves of the elder branch—of which, if you speak true, and I think that you do—you are the last twig. The women of my father's line are different in appearance, which was why I did not at first recognise you for what you are. It took the portrait of Lady Adelaide Cleeve to do that.'

Louise gave a half-laugh. 'Legitimate—or illegitimate—who is to know which at this late date?'

'Nevertheless,' said Marcus. 'Nothing has changed between us. Your honesty impresses me. Many in your position would have brazenly claimed legitimacy, but you have laid out the few facts of your past with an impartial clarity which would be applauded in a court of law. Whatever else, it seems that we are quite distant cousins. I can only wish that you were more than a cousin to me.'

Louise's heart gave a great leap. She was not to lose him—as she had thought possible.

'The thing is,' he went on, 'that while I can quite understand your desire to remain anonymous so far as this Sywell business is concerned, I think that your guardian, despite his care of you, did you few favours by not trying harder to establish your legitimacy—or rather by giving up the hunt so soon. He also did you the worst disservice by encouraging your marriage to Sywell.'

'All that may be true in hindsight,' said Louise. 'But now that you know my story, what do you intend to do about it?'

'Well, I shall certainly not broadcast it around London, you may be sure of that,' he told her. 'I don't believe that you murdered Sywell. I am sure that you can prove that you were safely here in London when he was killed. Nor has it changed my opinion of you. On the contrary, I am full of admiration for your resourcefulness, Louise. I hope that I may call you that. Madame Félice has suddenly become a figment, a fairy-tale figure behind which Louise Cleeve—or Hanslope—takes refuge.'

So he did understand. He had not called her Louise Cleeve, the daughter of a man who was properly a Viscount, but she never thought of herself as that. The Honourable Louise Cleeve was someone in a romance as she had earlier said, not the down-to-earth woman who made dresses.

Her eyes filled with tears. 'I am so relieved that you do not think me a liar,' she murmured. 'I would never have told you any of this if you had not seen my resemblance to the portrait in Berkeley Square.'

Marcus rose and came over to where she sat. He went down on one knee beside her, and touched her hand to try to reassure her. The look of pain on her face was affecting him strongly.

'My dear,' he said, lifting her hand and kissing it, although to do so was temptation itself, but only a cur would assail her with his love when she was so greatly distressed, 'my dear, you have been carrying such a monstrous burden for so long that I am amazed at the fortitude with which you have faced life. You have my deepest admiration. Now, I am going to ask you to allow me to do something to help you. I would like to consult Jackson, the ex-Runner, about your past, and ask him to try to find the proofs of your parents' marriage and your own birth. I would charge him to do so in the strictest confidence—which I am sure that he would honour.'

'No, indeed not. I do not wish anyone other than yourself to know this. My secrets must remain secrets.'

'Consider this, my dearest heart. In fairness to my father and myself, we must attempt to discover whether or not you are Louise Cleeve, the daughter of Lord Rupert Cleeve. That you might be makes no difference to the ownership of Steepwood, since the estate, like the title, was entailed on the male line. But you should not only take your rightful place in society, but you ought also to have the dowry which would rightly have been yours.'

'I don't want any of it,' she told him stubbornly. 'I am Louise Hanslope who is also Madame Félice, and that is all I wish to be. Even if this Sywell business were not hanging over me, I should still say the same. I don't want the whole world to gossip over my past.'

'To please me,' he said softly. 'You have suffered a great wrong—through no fault of me and mine, I own, but still a great wrong.'

He lifted himself a little and took her into his arms. The sensation was so sweet that Louise gave a low groan and almost surrendered to the light kisses he was favouring her cheek with until she stopped him by pulling away.

'No, Mr Marks, you are not to do that. It was not in our bargain. We are friends, not lovers.'

'But I want to be your friend and lover more than

ever now that I know that you are my distant cousin Louise. Say that you will allow me to speak to Jackson and permit him try to settle the matter once and for all.'

Louise shook her head. 'Mr Marks would obey me in this. Lord Angmering may do as he pleases. I cannot stop him, although I wish that I could.'

'You break my heart,' he whispered, but he made no attempt to take her in his arms again. She looked so desolate that all he wished to do was comfort her, and so he told her.

'And we both know how that might end,' she said sadly. 'There has been enough loose folly in the Cleeve family, enough members of it not troubling about tomorrow, without our adding to it. My father, and my grandfather between them brought me to this pass. Do not let us make matters worse.'

Marcus had to acknowledge the truth of this.

He bowed his head. He could not agree to what she wished, for he thought that later she might reconsider, when the shock of telling him her sad story had worn off.

So he said nothing, merely sat quietly and companionably at her feet hoping that his mere presence might calm her, and he thought that perhaps it did for he heard her breathing change.

Louise hardly knew herself. One part of her wanted to throw herself into Marcus's arms and forget everything she had ever lived by. In them she knew that she might find peace. But that peace would be temporary, and when the initial joy of her surrender was over she would be back from where she had started with nothing solved—and her honour surrendered.

The other part was thinking that she could not bear to confide in Jackson! The thought was horrible. She had learned early in life to trust no one and she certainly was not prepared to trust a predatory thief-taker. If she was doing him an injustice, then she would rather risk that than expose herself to the cruelly idle gossip which revelation of her true identity—whatever that was—would inevitably create.

She knew Marcus well enough to grasp that if he thought that it was in her interest to involve Jackson then he would not hesitate do so. He was plainly a man who was highly protective of anyone who was friend, family or lover. She would not plead with him, nor try to influence him, or play any of the womanly tricks to bend him to her will which she had seen other women employ.

Instead she finally said, rather drowsily, 'Mr Marks, have you no other duties to attend to?'

He looked up into her lovely face, admiring that firm and pretty chin from below. A chin which rightly told, not only of her strength of will, but also of her relationship with the senior branch of the Cleeves.

'None which is more important to me than caring for the woman I love. All else can wait—except...'

He did not finish and Louise said, a trifle ruefully, 'Except that you might wish to talk to Jackson as soon as possible. I would rather you did not.'

'It is in your interest,' he said simply.

Louise shrugged her shoulders. 'I find it difficult to believe that, after all these years, he could find something which my guardian could not.'

'Your guardian was not England's most experienced thief-taker and tracker-down of what many might think unconsidered trifles, and Jackson is.'

She had no answer to that, other than to change tack completely and ask, 'Would you care to stay and take nuncheon, Mr Marks?'

'With pleasure, Louise, my darling.'

So they ate nuncheon together before Marcus left, privately resolved to see Jackson immediately. It had taken all his strength for him to sit quietly opposite to her, eating and drinking when all the time what he really wanted to do was to take her in his arms and…

He told his body to behave itself and wondered if his love was feeling as calm as she looked. Did she burn for him as he burned for her? Was he overestimating her feelings for him? He hoped not.

What he did not know was that Louise's wish for him not to touch her owed everything to the fact that his mere touch was liable to undo her. Even the reverent kiss which he offered her hand when he left had the most powerful effect on her. If she had ever believed that she was a cold woman whom no man could affect, then meeting Marcus Angmering had taught her otherwise.

Chapter Five

Louise was not mistaken. Marcus had every intention of setting Jackson the task of trying to prove whether or not she was really Louise Cleeve. He made up his mind to visit the man at once, but he did not need to do so. He again entered Cleeve House to find Jackson on the point of leaving.

'You were looking for me?' he asked.

'No, I needed to speak to your pa again, but he is out.'

'Again?' queried Marcus, 'I thought that you were finished with him.'

'Oh, in my line of business we rarely finish with people until a crime is solved, and seeing that the Home Office are still urgent in this matter I must carry out my duty. Your pa's secretary has arranged an appointment for me. Now, what can I do for you, m'lord?—for I can see that your interest in me is most particular.'

Marcus gave a snort of laughter. 'Am I so transparent, or do you own a crystal ball, Jackson?'

'Oh, a man's manner tells many things about him, if one knows how to interpret it,' offered Jackson. 'No magic is needed there, m'lord.'

'Well, there's no denying it, I do wish to speak to you and urgently. But before I do so I must ask you to treat everything I am about to say to you with the utmost confidentiality—otherwise this interview is over.'

'You would wish me to buy a pig in a poke, m'lord? Come, come, that is not a possibility in my line of business.'

'Suppose half of what I am about to tell you would clear up one of your lines of enquiry in the Steepwood mystery, and that the other half has nothing to do with that—or the Home Office for that matter, what then? I am an honest man, Jackson, treat me as one and save yourself much future work.'

Jackson stared at him for some time without speaking before shrugging his shoulders and saying, 'Very well, m'lord—I trust that you are not bamming me because if you are—why then, look out, I say!'

'No bamming,' said Marcus. 'Now, come into the study, and I will tell you an interesting couple of stories.'

Jackson nodded. 'Very well, m'lord, but be short, I am a busy man.'

Marcus, as briefly as he could, began by telling him that Madame Félice had confessed to him that she was indeed Sywell's missing Marchioness, and also that she could prove conclusively from her shop accounts and the day-book her man of all work kept that she could not possibly have murdered her late husband, since she had been working in London at the critical time.

Jackson had fished his piece of paper out and was nodding over it while Marcus spoke. When he had finished, he said, 'Well, m'lord, you have confirmed what I already believed: that Madame *is* Sywell's widow and the friend of that pretty little fox, Miss Athene Filmer as was. They make a good pair. I already have reason to believe that Madame did not kill her husband and, furthermore, did not hire anyone else to do so.'

Marcus stared at him. 'Then, knowing this, why were you continuing to badger her?'

'Oh, dear, m'lord, you're a clever fellow. You ought to know that it's one thing for me to believe something, but until I have proof I have to continue to check and probe before going on to other lines which might lead nowhere because my belief was not correct. You follow me, I'm sure. Yes, we can write the lady off, but I would still wish her to tell me her story, not just have it at second-hand from you. Now, m'lord, what's the other problem you have?'

'Well, that concerns Madame, too,' and Marcus

recounted as plainly as he could the mystery of Louise's birth. 'What I would like you to do for me, if you would, is to try to trace any records which could prove, or disprove, her story.'

Jackson whistled. 'Interesting, m'lord, most interesting. So the guardian, you say—rather, she says—could find nothing at all. What she has told you might explain, if it is the truth, something about her marriage which has always puzzled me.'

He stopped and stared hard at Marcus. 'Think hard, m'lord—you are a man of the world—what is damned odd about the marriage, if you will pardon the expression.'

Marcus had never really thought about Sywell's marriage to the supposed daughter of his bailiff. If so, he might have concluded that it arose from a sort of whim on the part of a man whose judgement was already faulty. He was about to tell Jackson that when something else struck him.

He said slowly, working things out as he spoke, 'Sywell was a damned debauched rogue, and when he married was already impotent—so why did he marry her at all? He may have been a rogue but he wasn't a fool. He always looked after his own interests and be damned to everyone else. One might have spoken of it as softening of the brain, but are you thinking that there was more to it than that?'

'Aye, m'lord. You have just told me that Madame might be a Cleeve, part of the family which Sywell had spent his life destroying. Think, m'lord, think.

Hanslope might have given her secret away without meaning to, to Sywell himself or to his creature and by-blow, Burneck, who kept watch on everything for his master if he is to be believed. So, if the girl is a Cleeve, what a splendid joke it would be to marry her, in order to gloat over having a hold over yet another member of the family. What, too, if he knew of, or had acquired, evidence that would prove her identity? Imagine his delight in tormenting and maltreating her while he hugged that knowledge to him? Oh, yes, that marriage has always puzzled me—and I believe that I may have lighted on a possible explanation of its mystery.'

'It's a bit of a leap in logic,' said Marcus thoughtfully, 'but it jibes with what we know of Sywell.'

'Aye, that it does, and think, there may still be evidence in existence. Oh, yes, m'lord, I'll take on your commission. I've wanted to have another go at Burneck, the man's nearly as big an offence against nature as his late master, that he is. If I do find anything it won't solve Sywell's murder, but I believe I'm getting near to doing that as well.'

'And you will keep what I have told you confidential—about Madame being Sywell's widow?'

'Oh, indeed, she's out of the reckoning now, no need to put the poor lady into the way of more trouble.'

'Indeed,' said Marcus in a heartfelt voice. 'Her life has been one long trouble, it is time that she had some happiness in it, some relief from perpetual worry. Once she has told you her story, and you are happy with it, I would like you to inform her, if you would, that you will keep her secret and will not need to trouble her again.'

'Very well, m'lord. Leave matters to me.'

'Thank you,' said Marcus, shaking him by the hand but wondering wryly what Louise was going to think of him for having spoken to Jackson after all—even if the result was going to be that she was no longer suspected of having murdered Sywell. Perhaps she would forgive him when he told her that Jackson had agreed to try to trace the evidence that would bring her out of the shadows.

The only trouble was that if she were a Cleeve then his continual offers to make her his mistress must have seemed a gross insult to her, and he could scarcely continue to chase after that hare. On the other hand, and Marcus gave a slow grin at the mere idea: Why not make her my wife? After all, even before I knew that she was a Cleeve I was toying with the notion of offering for her.

I should lose my bet with Jack and look a boastful fool into the bargain—but what of that: I should be uniting the two branches of the family and gaining myself a nonpareil as well. Few women could have survived such a childhood and on top of that have managed to make themselves a tidy little fortune as well.

Yes, as soon as all this is safely behind us I shall make an offer for her, and settle down at last. The prospect so entranced him that walking upstairs he allowed the Two Neds to halloo by him without even noticing that they were there.

'Speak to Jackson again?' exclaimed Louise. 'But why? You have told him everything about me which concerns him.'

'He has his duty to do,' explained Marcus. 'What I told him was hearsay—yours will be direct evidence of which he can take due note.'

'And he will make nothing public, you say—no tattling to anyone of who Madame Félice really is.'

'He agreed to that, but my darling, you do realise that if he proves beyond a doubt that you are legally my cousin Rupert's daughter, that will inevitably have to be made known if you are to resume your true name.'

Louise shuddered. 'Will this never be over? I feel that I am walking through my life looking over my shoulder at what has gone before. I want, I need, a present and a future. I scarcely know what my true name is.'

They were on their way to Chelsea's autumn fair, not a venue where they might expect to meet anyone who knew them. Marcus was wearing his clerk's outfit and Louise looked like her little maid on an outing and did not resemble in the slightest that elegant *modiste,* Madame Félice. She was wearing a simple blue and white print dress, stout black shoes, a plain straw bonnet with a blue band, and an anonymous light shawl, for London and its outlying districts were experiencing an Indian summer, and the sun was hot upon them.

'I don't give a farthing for what your true name is,' Marcus declared. 'You are my dear Louise and that is quite enough for me.'

'But I do,' fretted Louise. 'After all, you have no need to worry about such things. You are Marcus Angmering, heir to that Lord of All, the Earl of Yardley, so you can afford to dismiss such matters as trifling. I, on the other hand, have no notion of whether I am legitimate or illegitimate, and I should dearly like to know which state I might claim to be. Even to be sure that I am neither a Cleeve nor legitimate would be better than not knowing whether I am fish, flesh, fowl or good red herring.'

Marcus gave a shout of laughter. 'All my favourite foods, my darling, so even less reason for you to worry. Now smile, we are on our way to enjoy ourselves and forget tomorrow. I have the notion that you have never had much enjoyment in your life and I intend to see that you have a plentiful supply of it in the future.'

This did bring a smile to her face. 'I'm sorry for being grumpy,' she said. 'And I suppose that, so long as he keeps to his promise to be confidential, you were right to speak to Jackson. I am being ungrateful, am I not?'

'Understandable under the circumstances,' said Marcus cheerfully. 'Now, seeing that we have reached the fair, why don't I pay for you to visit one of the fortune-tellers? She, or he—there are some hes—might solve all your problems in a trice. Which do you prefer, crystal balls, palm readings or tarot cards? I am sure that they are all on offer.'

'Well,' said Louise dryly, 'it might be as useful as anything which Jackson could find after all this time, so yes to that—so long as you agree to play Find the Lady. In view of our circumstances, rather apt, don't you think, Mr Marks?'

'Excellent,' Marcus replied, 'but don't expect me to win at cards—I have had such good luck in finding my particular lady—and you know the old saying, lucky at cards, unlucky in love, and I suppose that works in reverse at well.'

His reward was the first heartfelt laugh he had ever heard from Louise, and into the bargain she did what other young girls were doing with their swains—she slipped her hand into the crook of his arm.

The idea of Marcus being a swain amused her, and so she told him.

'Hmm,' he said thoughtfully. 'I always thought that swains were rustic creatures with a straw in their mouths, not lawyers' clerks on holiday. I believe that we are known as pen-pushers.'

This earned him another laugh and Marcus began to think that things were really looking up if his darling could enjoy herself and forget her cares. It turned out that Louise had never been to a fair before, and Marcus had certainly not attended one in his character as Mr Marks. He liked the idea of being a nobody on holiday among other nobodies, but he was honest enough to admit to himself that he would probably not like being one for life. This profound thought served to increase his admiration of Louise's feat in transforming herself from nothing into a person of consequence.

What made Louise happy was that no one stared at them, nor remarked upon them at all. She did not have to remember who she was, but simply enjoyed herself, her delicate arm tucked into Marcus's strong one. He insisted on buying her a toffee-apple, to which she only agreed when he promised to buy himself oysters from the next booth they came to— and eat them in the street.

'And I'll have a toffee-apple as well, to keep you company,' he announced magnanimously, and Marcus, Lord Angmering, known for his strict adherence to all the proprieties, walked along chewing away at an apple on a stick, between the booths which offered everything from a captive mermaid in a tank, to fairings ranging from ribbons and cockades to cheap china busts of the King and the Prince Regent, to representations of nymphs and shepherds. He could not have done anything more calculated to win his beloved's heart.

Next Louise bought him a cockade to wear in his shabby hat, and, in return he stumped up for a bunch of blue ribbons—'to bind up your bonny fair hair,' he half-sang to her, altering the words of the old ballad to fit Louise's red-tinged golden locks when he handed them over. Singing in the street—even if so low that only she might hear—what next would he do? wondered Louise, who, like Marcus, had never enjoyed herself so much for years.

What next, indeed? Next turned out to be the fortune-teller. This one offered everything from crystal balls to tarot cards—'You pays your money and you takes your choice,' was painted in crude words across the front of a canvas tent.

'I'll pay,' announced Marcus, to be met with, 'No, I will,' from Louise and they had a friendly wrangle in the entrance to the booth, to the delight of the small girl who was collecting entrance money.

Inside was dark and somewhat smelly. The smell came from a few candles burning in the gloom. The fortune-teller was a gypsy woman, rather elderly, with a face like a witch in a painting which hung in the corridor at Cleeve House in London.

She stared at the pair of them and said in a deep voice, 'You've paid for one only, so I take it that it's the lady who wishes to know her future.'

'Yes,' said Louise, staring at the crystal ball on the table between her and the gypsy woman. Beside the ball rested several packs of tarot cards, a bowl of clear water, and something which looked like a magician's wand.

'And which do you choose, m'lady?'

Louise said, to Marcus's amusement, for, all unknowingly, she had assumed Madame Félice's haughty tones, 'Why do you address me as m'lady?'

The woman leaned forward and said 'Come, come, you are m'lady, are you not? Do you think to deceive me by wearing the clothes of a servant?'

Louise, flabbergasted, stared back at her, and then, in a most unladylike manner, jerked her thumb at Marcus, and her manners having deserted her completely, asked, 'And him? What about him?'

Without turning her head to look at him the woman smiled and said softly, 'Why, he's an even bigger fraud than you are. Is this a prank you are engaged in? A prank designed to trick me, so that you might go home to boast to the quality of how you unmasked the gypsy fortune-teller? If so, you must do better than this.'

Marcus, who had been listening to her, his face a picture—although what sort of picture he might have found it difficult to say—now spoke.

'You are right, madame—and yet you are also wrong. Unriddle me that.'

She looked straight at him for the first time. 'Oh, my fine gentleman who has never worked in an office in his life, do you hope to trick *me* with such a question.'

She put her hands over her eyes before dropping them and saying, 'I am right that you are quality, so why are you dressed as though you are not? Is it possible that you have put on your false clothes to deceive the world rather than me? That you entered my tent on a whim and not by design?'

'Oh, bravo,' said Marcus softly. 'And now let me unriddle *you* a little. I am dressed as a clerk, but I betray nothing of what a true clerk is. My cuffs are neither frayed nor ink-stained, my poor stock is clean and new, and has not been laundered so many times that it is frayed. My hands betray none of the signs that I spend the day with a quill pen in them. My nails are clean and my writing finger is uncallused.

'Shall I go on? Or shall I inform you how you know that I am a gentleman and that my companion is not a servant. Oh, I forgot our manner... Everything you have told us so far is the result of careful observation, there is nothing magic about it.'

The gypsy woman did something strange. She threw back her head and began to laugh. 'Oh, you are a rare one, you are. Everyone who meets you tends to underestimate you. They think that because you are straightforward you are not clever—and cunning—tell me how I know *that* simply by looking at you?'

Marcus shook his head. 'No, no, you have not only looked at me, you have heard me speak. Now, scry for my companion—I believe that is the phrase—and tell me of her future, something which you could not guess simply by looking at us and speaking to us. I am willing to pay you to use all of the tools of your trade, if that is what you call it.'

'Oh, I like you, m'lord, as I believe you to be. I wish I had met you when I was as young and pretty as your lady is, we could have had a rare time together. Does she know how lucky she is going to be when she shares your bed?'

Louise blushed, and, adopting her Madame Félice voice again, for it was pointless trying to pretend to be her own servant, said, 'I came here to have my fortune told, pray tell it.'

'You're a fair match for him, I see,' said the woman. 'Give me your hand, dearie, we'll begin with that.'

Louise laid her hand palm up on the table. The woman peered hard at it saying, 'Ah, yes, you are a lady, but not yet a lady. I cannot tell from this what your future might be, for it is strange, but not as strange as your past. Your hand tells me of that and little more—which is passing wonderful. Should you wish to learn your future then I must look in the crystal—do you wish to learn your future, lady? Many do not.'

'Yes,' said Louise swiftly, before she could change her mind. 'I am tired of contemplating my past—I would learn of my future if possible.'

'Then keep your hand in mine, for you have a power which few possess: and that is to prevent anyone from truly knowing you if you are minded not to allow them to. That is why your hand is closed to me. Open your heart to me, lady, and I may be able to help you.'

Louise nodded agreement and tried to reveal herself to the woman before her. The gypsy muttered some words before looking deep into the crystal.

Suddenly, however, she threw Louise's hand from her with a guttural cry, exclaiming, 'No, your past is so powerful that it insists on being known. Blood, lady, you are surrounded by blood—but none of it is yours, nor have you shed it. All those whom you most dearly loved were taken from you. Your father you never knew, he died in blood not long after you were born. You had a husband who was no husband—I cannot see him—I only know that blood surrounds him, too.'

She cried out again, before adding, 'Let me rest a moment, for you have tired me greatly. I think that I can see that you have a future, and a long one, but it is dim.'

Marcus's mouth twitched. He had been trying not to smile at what he thought was a fine old piece of pantomime, until the gypsy spoke of Louise's husband who was no husband, and of the blood which surrounded both him and her. He saw that his love's face had grown pale and for a moment thought of taking her away from someone whom he had earlier decided was a charlatan and trickster—but now he did not know what she was.

Except that Louise made no effort to rise, or to leave—and the decision must be hers, after all. The gypsy was stirring again. She had begun to mutter words in a language which neither Marcus, nor Louise, knew.

'I have broken the spell which binds you,' she said, reverting to her accented English. 'It was laid on you and yours long ago—and it is on him, too,' she added, pointing at Marcus. 'It curses you both because what you inherited was sacred and was stolen from those who raised it and false gods put in its place. Now, I will look again in my crystal in order to discover whether, having banished it, I may read your destiny more plainly.'

She took Louise's hand again, and this time recited a form of words, again in that strange language, before she looked deep into the ball before her.

'Yes,' she exclaimed, 'there is something there, it is still dim, but I can read a little of what the magic is trying to tell me. Alas, it is not clear, it is still vague and distant so that I have nothing detailed to tell you. All I can say is that you will gain your heart's desire. What you have been looking for all of your life you will also surely find, although I cannot plainly see what that is. It involves a name and a great house—a strange house—and there your joint destinies lie. More, I cannot tell you. Your will is strong, lady, and I needed to subdue it to see even the little I have.'

She relinquished Louise's hand and lay back in her intricately carved chair panting as though she had run a race.

'Oh, I am so tired. To break the spell which binds you both was a feat almost beyond my endurance.

'This spell,' asked Marcus, intrigued even though he still thought that the old woman was making this whole farrago up—and even though she had spoken truly of some parts of Louise's past. 'This spell, Madame, to what does it relate?'

'All I can tell you is that there is a Grove which was called Sacred which was despoiled long ago, and they who live in and own it will suffer from a curse placed upon them by the original owners, a curse which will ruin their lives so that they will rarely know happiness. Far away from it, some might find contentment. More than that I cannot say—other than that I have lifted it from you and your lady, so that you may live long and happy lives.'

Both Marcus and Louise were thinking of Steepwood's Sacred Grove, and of the ruined lives of all those who had ever owned the Abbey and the grounds in which the grove was situated. It was not until his father had left England—and the grove— behind that he had found happiness in India.

He half-began to ask the gypsy whether she could lift the curse altogether, but true child of the Age of Reason that he was, he found himself inwardly laughing at such an absurd notion.

Yet the old woman had said so much that was true.

Louise had begun to stir. She had been shocked

by what the gypsy had told her. She said, her voice low, for she was still distressed by what she had both seen and heard. 'You said that I would be happy, and that I would find that for which I have always wished. Can I believe you?'

The old woman's smile was weary. 'I can only tell you what I saw—and hope that you and your man will find in the future the happiness which you seek. Time alone will prove me right or wrong, but I believe that the crystal told me true.'

She looked Marcus straight in the eye, saying, 'You do not trust me, young sir, because you are limited by your cleverness. You only believe in what you can see, hear and touch, not in the something more than that which lies around us and which we can only dimly understand, if at all.'

Marcus rose and bowed to her, and acknowledged what she had just said. He spoke without mockery, quoting from Shakespeare's play, *Hamlet*. 'There are more things in Heaven and Earth, Horatio, than are dreamed of in your philosophy.'

'Exactly so, young fellow. Leave me now. I may scry no more this afternoon. You brought a strong and evil power in with you, and that power has gone, but it was heavy work for me to rid you of it, heavy work.'

They were outside again, blinking in the orange sunlight of an early October afternoon. Louise said, her voice faltering a little, 'Are we to believe all that, Mr Marks?'

Marcus turned around and slipped an arm around her shoulders. For the first time since he had met her she looked frail and wan. He gave her a reassuring hug, careless of passing watchers. After all, a young clerk might hug his sweetheart in the street, might he not? The constraints which bound Marcus Cleeve did not obtain here.

'I don't know,' he said. 'I thought her a fraud at first, but later…I find later difficult to explain. All that talk about blood, and then the Sacred Grove and the curse of which we both know…'

'Exactly,' said Louise, echoing the gypsy's last words to them. 'How could she know of that? And the Abbey—the strange building she called it, and so it is being religious house and home combined. You must admit that was frightening. I agreed with you when you told her that she could guess that we were not working people because to an observant eye everything about us betrays our true station—but the rest—how did she know that?'

'Louise,' Marcus said gravely. 'Try not to think too much about what she told you. Or, if you must, believe what she said at the end.'

'About our future happiness?'

'Yes, you were speaking of the future earlier this afternoon. Try to believe that she spoke truly. Look, I do believe that the roses are already returning to your cheeks, my dear Miss Louise. Keep them there and I promise to eat oysters again if you will eat jellied eels! How is that for a great concession on my part?'

'Dear Mr Marks,' said Louise, who after the strangeness of their recent experience had forgotten that she was supposed to be holding Marcus off, not encouraging him. 'Dear Mr Marks, how kind you are. Yes, I will eat jellied eels though I have never done so before and hope that they will not make me feel sick!'

Nor did they. Eating from their paper screws full of fishy delicacies Marcus and his love found it possible to forget past and future, and enjoy the mindless present which was Chelsea Fair.

'Blasted Northamptonshire, and bloody Steepwood,' grumbled Jackson aloud. 'It would be raining again.'

He had come hot-foot from London, which he considered to be the only civilised place in the Kingdom, and was bound for the cottage in Steep Ride where Solomon Burneck now lodged.

It would be a pleasure to upset the surly bastard once more. It quite made this whole tedious business worthwhile.

The cottage was at the end of a muddy lane leading off an equally muddy by-way. Jackson watched from a distance until he saw the landlady leave—he wanted no witnesses to what he was about to do. Burneck himself opened the door and made a disagreeable face at him.

'What, you again!'

Almost the same words as Marcus Angmering had used, but the tone was very different.

'That's right,' Jackson said, 'regular bad penny, aren't I? Let me in, will you, this rain's damned wet.'

'Why should I?' asked Burneck. 'You've no right…'

'This is my right,' said Jackson, 'and a damned useful one it is, too.' And he put a hard and horny hand on Burneck's chest and pushed him into the cottage's small front room.

'Hey, damn that,' spluttered Burneck. 'I haven't invited you in and an Englishman's home is his castle.'

'Number one,' said Jackson. 'This isn't your home, you're only a lodger, and number two, it's not a castle, so I can do as I please. Is the Missis in?'

'Yes,' lied Burneck.

'Now there's a lying tale to begin with,' grinned Jackson, 'for I saw her leave with her shopping basket not five minutes ago.'

'She'll be back any moment.' Burneck sounded desperate.

'If she does, and I doubt it, I'll tell her that you're gallows-meat I'm hauling off to the County gaol. So now you can take me upstairs and we can have a cosy little chat.'

'What for? You know that I had nothing to do

with my pa's death. Why should I kill him? I've lost room and board and my position in life.'

Jackson began to laugh.

'Your position in life! What's that? The place where you're beneath everyone's feet and consideration?'

He slammed the door behind him, saying, 'Now, you piece of low-life filth, tell me all that you know about the Marchioness, Miss Louise Hanslope as was. I've a burning curiosity about the lady, seeing that Sywell chose to marry her when he was a ripe piece of spoiled beef.'

'His choice, not mine,' grumbled Burneck. 'Can't imagine what you want to know about her for.'

'Well, I'm after wondering why Sywell married her at all—his bailiff's adopted daughter, wasn't she? Now, what I want you to tell me is who she was before Hanslope adopted her.'

'And how the devil should I know that? I've no idea.'

Jackson grabbed him by the collar. 'Why is it that I don't believe you? Tell me the truth, damn you. Tell me all about the child Hanslope brought here out of nowhere, and tell me why your master, who always had an eye for the main chance, married her. What main chance was he thinking of when he did such an odd thing? Knowing Sywell's reputation, there must have been something in it for him.'

Burneck began to shake his head. 'I don't know…'

Jackson took him by the throat this time and breathed ale fumes into his victim's purpling face.

'Keep mum, you lying wretch, and I'll run you in for Sywell's murder, that I will.'

'You wouldn't do that. You know that I didn't do it,' Burneck croaked desperately.

'Wouldn't I just! My masters want this business ended and don't care how it's done. I could end it tomorrow by fitting you up as the murderer. You'd do as well as another. Save yourself by telling me about Sywell and the girl. Otherwise…'

Burneck began to babble at him, his eyes wild. 'Let me go, then. If I have your word that you'll leave me alone if I talk, I'll tell you everything. After all, what's to lose, if I do? They're all dead but the girl.'

'Exactly—now talk. And I want the truth, the whole truth and nothing but the truth or you'll be in the dock at the Old Bailey.'

'It was when Johnny Hanslope came to my pa and said that his sister was dying and he had to go to Cheltenham to see her safely buried and to bring her little girl back with him. M'lord said he could go, grudging-like, and when Johnny had gone to make ready for the journey I told M'lord that to my certain knowledge he had no sister, and what was he doing pretending that he had one and going all the way to Cheltenham to rescue her?

'M'lord always loved a puzzle and he liked to know everything about those who worked for him.

Knowledge was power, he always told me. He gave a great laugh and said, ''Follow Johnny there and find out what he's up to. Perhaps it's nothing but an old mistress of his and her by-blow, but we might as well know. Don't let him twig you're after him, though.'''

'Just like that, eh?' queried Jackson, who was beginning to be intrigued by this tale and was also amused by the way Sywell alternated between being Pa and M'lord to his bastard son.

'Aye, he was bored, you know. So I ups and follows Johnny to Cheltenham, and true enough there was a dying woman and a little girl. I took rooms at the local inn and made a few discreet enquiries. What really interested me was that the dying woman was a Frenchie. What was Johnny Hanslope doing with a Frenchwoman? She had a funny name, too.

'So, I watched the house and one morning Johnny came out with the kid and walked over to a neighbour who I'd been told was giving him and the girl dinner. After a short time he walked back into the village. So I entered the house by the back way, and searched it. Upstairs I found the Frenchwoman lying on the bed—quite dead, but still warm. I suppose that he'd gone to fetch the laying-out nurse.'

Burneck stopped and offered Jackson a knowing grin: from not wanting to tell his story he now seemed to be enjoying doing so—a phenomenon which Jackson had often seen.

'The thing was—and I can tell you it really

knocked me flying—that I knew her. I'd seen her years before when Lord Rupert Cleeve had secretly visited Johnny Hanslope. How she had arrived in Cheltenham with their child was a mystery. There had been a rumour that Lord Rupert had married a Frenchwoman—some said that he'd only pretended to marry her—whatever the truth, here she was, dead, and Johnny Hanslope had her kid.

'It occurred to me that she might be carrying proof of her marriage, if there had been a marriage—and the child's birth, and that my pa would be pleased as punch if I stole them for him so that Johnny couldn't take the child to Lord Yardley. Besides, to bastardise one of the Cleeves would be the sort of caper he'd like, anyways.'

'Aye, and the idea pleased you, too, didn't it, Burneck, didn't it?'

'If you say so. So I searched her belongings— there weren't many—and found her marriage certificate and the record of the kid's birth as well as her diary. I took them and scarpered. I was right about M'lord—he laughed fit to bust, he did, and hung on to them. Johnny never even knew I'd been there. Pa often had a good laugh about it when he was drunk, and when the kid grew up and became a beauty he laughed even harder when he married her, though he was past everything by then, poor devil.'

Devil certainly, but hardly poor—who could pity Sywell, thought Jackson grimly. What he said was,

'Why have you stopped? What happened to the papers when Sywell was murdered and went to Hell?'

Burneck put his finger by his nose. 'Aye, well, I knew where he kept his secrets. Them as was sent to solve his murder went through the Abbey and never found his hiding-places, but if they'd done so they'd have found nothing, because I'd been there before them.' He laughed hard at his own cleverness.

'So *you* have them now?' asked Jackson. 'First you steal them for Sywell, and then for yourself. What did you propose to do with them?'

'Knowledge is power, they might come in useful some day.' And this time he offered Jackson a wink.

'Not to you, they won't,' said Jackson, grinning again, 'for if you don't hand them over to me I'll haul you before the nearest beak for theft—because that wasn't all you lifted from Sywell, was it?'

'Oh, I knew you'd cheat me,' howled Burneck. 'Never trust a Runner, I should have known better.'

'Dear, dear,' said Jackson. 'Give me the legal papers and the diary and you can keep the rest, by the look of them they're not worth much.'

'Only things to remind me of my poor pa—you can have the papers—I'll fetch them for you.'

'Big of you,' said Jackson, 'seeing that I would have taken them from you without your kind assistance. I want to look at your other booty, too, in case there is anything there that will help me solve your poor, dear pa's murder. I'm sure you'd want that.'

Burneck gave up. He pointed to a battered trunk in the corner of the room, and handed Jackson its key. 'At the bottom,' he almost groaned, 'inside a Bible my pa once gave me.'

'Sywell gave you a Bible,' exclaimed the entranced Jackson, throwing out grubby clothing and a couple of tarnished silver candlesticks in order to find it. Sure enough, there were the papers and the diary which told the truth of Louise's birth, but the Bible interested him, too. It was an old one, the King James version bound in scuffed and battered leather, and had an inscription in the front: Philip Cleeve, his book, it said, 1642.

'A bit of Sywell's loot,' said Jackson, putting the papers back inside it. 'I think Lord Yardley might like his property back.'

'No!' Burneck shrieked. 'It's all I have left of me dad!'

'Who stole it from its owner. Console yourself with your happy memories of the dear departed,' said Jackson nastily, 'and be grateful I don't haul you off to Newgate for stealing the rest of the stuff in the trunk, which I would, if it were worth anything.'

He laughed to himself as he walked downstairs to the sound of Burneck's lamentations. Well, at least M'lord Angmering was going to be happy with what he had found and that was all that concerned him.

And now for home. Dear old London, it might smell bad, but it was still better than these dead and alive holes scattered around the Shire counties!

'Marcus,' said his stepmother that same morning, 'I would be grateful for a private word with you, if you could spare a moment.'

'Always ready to spare a moment for you, my dear Marissa,' he said gallantly. He thought that she seemed worried, and he also thought that he could guess what was troubling her.

He was right. Once they had reached her pretty little sitting-room, where they were unlikely to be interrupted, she came to the point at once. Marissa had many practical virtues and was nearly as forthright as Marcus and his father: something which they both valued more than showy good looks, which were often associated with an empty head.

'It's your father, Marcus. He is not well—oh, I mean more than that his advanced years are afflicting him, that is to be expected—but after a fashion which troubles me. I think that he has some deep worry which is preventing him from sleeping and which is ruining his appetite. Have you any notion what can be wrong? More to the point, perhaps, have you noticed any change in his manner recently—or am I imagining things?'

'Dear Marissa,' he said, 'I don't think that you are. I, too, have been perturbed about him recently. To say that he does not seem himself is an understatement. He is very much *not* himself. True, he and I have achieved a *rapprochement* which I once would never have thought possible, but even that does not appear to have made him happy. It has made me so, but not him.'

Marissa nodded thoughtfully. 'True, he told me of it, and I agree with you. I have asked him if there is anything troubling him and he has been unusually brusque in denying any such thing. It occurred to me that it might be something which he did not care to confide to me because I am a woman, or because he does not want to trouble me, so I wonder if I could ask a favour of you...' She paused.

Marcus said, 'You would wish me to speak to him?'

'Oh, if only you would. He's such a punctilious man, you see, and it's passing strange that he's keeping a secret from me. We've always told one another our troubles, and this secrecy is most unlike him. I do know that that ex-Runner who keeps popping up has the power to distress him, but why should that be?'

'You need not worry about him,' Marcus assured her. 'He's been coming to see me rather than father—I've asked him to do an errand for me. On second thoughts, perhaps it's only because I have been refusing to marry that has been distressing him.'

His stepmother shook her head. 'Oh, he's spoken of that to me at length—and by the by, he has my full support. You would make a splendid husband and father.'

'But I'd be pushing the two Neds out of line,' protested Marcus.

'Oh, pooh to that. The dowry I brought with me will give them a good start in life, and when I look at the history of the Earls of Yardley I'm not sure that I would wish the title on either of them. Now, you, Marcus, are a different kettle of fish. You are a strong man, stronger even than your father—and I know that you'd look after my darlings. You look after everyone and everything, don't you? Even that pretty *modiste,* Madame Félice whom you've been meeting secretly!'

Marcus gave a great moan. 'Now how the devil— forgive me, my dear—do you know about that?'

'That tattling fool Jack Perceval has been spreading gossip about seeing you with her in Chelsea. If it weren't that she is a *modiste* I'd say she would make a good Lady Yardley, and encourage you to offer for her, but marrying out of one's class is never a good notion.'

Marcus shook his head. 'I don't really think that whether or not I marry is worrying him so much that he is looking ill. After all, there are always the Two Neds to fall back on—even if you're not too happy about one of them becoming the next Lord Yardley. I promise you that I'll try to winkle out of father what's troubling him, but you know how stubborn he is—if he wants to keep mum he will.'

'Oh, but you're even more stubborn than he is, so my money is on you. Don't let me down, will you?'

What could he say but that he wouldn't, although it was simply one more thing for him to worry about. As for Madame Félice being out of his class—well perhaps Jackson might have the answer to that when he came back from Steepwood. Then he might think about marriage. What was the old saying? 'Better marry than burn!'

Well, he was certainly burning, so marriage, either in or out of his class, was becoming to look more and more attractive.

Chapter Six

Louise could scarcely wait for the weekend to arrive so that she might meet Marcus, no, Mr Marks again. She had visited Berkeley Square once more, to fit out the Countess this time, but he had not been present. Sophia had said something about Marcus having gone to visit an old school friend in Surrey, but he had told her that he hoped to be back in London by Friday at the latest.

One odd thing about the visit was that when she was showing Sophia a new idea for a small crown of silk flowers to wear on her wedding day she had caught Lady Yardley watching her with an odd look on her face.

Now, what could all that be about? Marcus had not told her that Jack Perceval had seen them in Chelsea, for he had not wanted her to worry overmuch about the gossip that would inevitably follow. All the same, Louise worried a little about such a close inspection before telling herself sternly not to see a bear behind every bush. On the other hand, she had survived her unhappy start in life by using her intuition, which had frequently told her much about the people around her—often things which they did not want known.

The only time that her intuition had failed her was when she had agreed to marry Sywell. Thinking about Sywell made her remember her late guardian, and that brought her back again to what Jackson might, or might not, be finding when he started his search for her origins.

Which simply served as an excuse to think of Marcus who had hired him. Marcus, whom she now knew that she loved. Oh, if only they could meet more often, and on equal terms! She hated playing out a charade of the Prince and the beggar-maid with him, even though he tried to lighten that aspect of their relationship by calling himself Mr Marks.

Dear Mr Marks! She was still thinking this when she returned to Bond Street to find Lady Leominster and her suite present in full cry. The lady was demanding a new wardrobe and had been unhappy to find Madame absent.

'I hear that you've been visiting the Yardleys,' she carolled. 'Of course, Sharnbrook is biting the bullet at last, is he not? Such a dear girl, Sophia, I hope that you are doing her proud, Madame. Oh, yes, we never thought Sharnbrook would be leg-shackled, and now that he's gone, one supposes Angmering will be the next.'

'Oh, m'lady,' simpered one of her toadies who had been given the lady's reticule to guard. 'Have you not heard? He has bet Jack Perceval that he will not marry during the next year. Of all things he said that…' she crimsoned a little, but her patron, never one to be mealy-mouthed, said forcefully, 'Spit it out, my dear. I'm sure that Madame will not be troubled if you are over-frank—after all, she is French, and we all know what they are like.'

'Well, he said that he preferred having an arrangement, if you take my meaning, since the lady who agreed to one would be less demanding than a wife—or something like that…'

'Spoken like a man,' said the lady, giving Louise a glance which could only be interpreted as meaningful. 'One hears that he has found such a lady—I wonder, who can it be?'

She did not intend to be malicious, merely to enjoy herself and her domination of all around her. Louise took the opportunity to hide her crimsoning face by kneeling down to pin up the gown in which her forewoman had dressed the lady before she had arrived from her visit to the Yardleys. She said, her voice muffled, 'I really have no notion, m'lady. Your guess is as good as mine.'

Far from annoying society's dictator, this amused her. She had been told the night before, in confidence by Jack Perceval that he had reason to believe that Angmering had taken up with that *modiste*,

Madame Félice. Such bare-faced lying was to be admired.

She bent down and hissed sweetly into Louise's ear, 'Oh, I'm sure that you know better than that, m'dear, but I wish you well. Angmering's an admirable fellow but eccentric. Mum's the word, eh?'

Louise straightened up, stood back, and said, 'I don't think that that colour suits you, m'lady, too garish. Would you not prefer another shade? A delicate mauve would be better than purple.'

If a lady could be said to wink, then Lady Leominster did. 'Oh, I defer to you always, Madame, such discretion, and such taste. You may always dress me in future. That wretched woman I have been using has been making me look like a gypsy at a fair.'

Gypsies at fairs reminded Louise of Marcus, Lord Angmering, who made nasty bets with nasty people like Jack Perceval. She would never call him Mr Marks again. Mr Marks would not pursue poor girls in order to ruin them and win his shameless bet. Lord Angmering, on the other hand, was apparently capable of anything. Just wait until he came visiting again this Saturday. To use the kind of language that that supposed high and mighty lady had just been employing: she would give him what for and no mistake!

Saturday had come and Marcus was all impatience. He had arrived back in Berkeley Square early on Friday morning, and late in the afternoon Jackson had arrived, bursting with news. Marcus had heard him out, and could only regret that he had to wait until morning to tell Louise that she was well and truly Louise Cleeve, and possessed the means of proving it.

For some reason, though, when he arrived in Chelsea the little maid showed him into an empty room and told him that Madame was busy and would join him once she was free.

He had never felt so impatient in all his life, and after half an hour had dragged by he rose to his feet and paced the room agitatedly, although it was scarcely big enough to satisfy his urgent demand for action.

Finally the door opened and his beloved entered. Instead of offering him her usual happy greeting, however, she impaled him with a fixed stare, and said coldly, 'Well, m'lord, what is it this time that you come so early?'

'Mr Marks,' he told her smiling, for he half-thought that she must be playing a game with him, her manner to him being so different.

'Mr Marks?' queried Louise. 'Now, who may he be? I do not know him—and I think that you do not, m'lord.'

Marcus could no longer deceive himself. Something had happened which had revived the haughty creature whom he had first met. All the playful banter which had enlivened their recent meetings had quite disappeared. He moved towards her to try to take her hand, but she retreated from him, the hand upraised to repel him.

'What is it?' he asked her. 'What have I done? What has caused you to treat your dear Mr Marks so unkindly? I thought that we had become friends, nay, more than friends.'

'How can you ask such questions?' she told him, her face still frozen, 'when I learn that the *on dit* is that not only have you bet that you will never marry, but that you have also proclaimed that an arrangement with a willing woman would be far better. Almost immediately afterwards I discovered that it is all over London society that you are meeting me secretly. That gossiping gorgon Lady Leominster made it quite plain that she knew that we were doing so, and had the gall to twit me with it.'

What he had feared when Marissa had spoken to him of his meeting Louise had come to pass. Regardless of everything, the moment he had discovered that, he should have gone straight to Bond Street to tell her that their secret was a secret no more. Instead he had stupidly hoped that if he said nothing then it was unlikely that, living outside that society, she would ever find out.

He might have known what gossips many society hostesses were, the Leominster creature being the worst of them. She had probably deliberately let Louise know what was being said in order to mischief-make between them. If so, she had succeeded.

'My dear,' he said, 'I have never lied to you. I told you that I wanted you for my mistress—and that the choice was yours. As for the ton knowing that we are meeting, they did not learn that from me, but from that ineffable nodcock, Jack Perceval. What's more, once you had told me that you did not wish to have a liaison with me I have treated you with as much respect as I would treat my own sister, Sophia—nay, more, for I have always twitted and teased her insufferably, something which I have never done to you. Dear Miss Louise, forgive your cavalier for what he has not done, particularly when he comes to you with such splendid news.'

Louise stared at him. Could she believe him? The trouble was that she knew how unscrupulously the aristocracy and gentry often pursued those well below them in station. She had comforted more than one green young sempstress who had been betrayed by an upper-class lover. They would say anything to gain their ends, and then they would walk away, having deprived their victim of her virtue, or, at the worst, having left her with a bastard child as well as a ruined name.

She had vowed that she would never be such a fool, and until she met Marcus she had never been tempted to be one.

'Am I to believe you?' she asked him, her face softening a little. 'Or are you treating me with such care, such kind consideration, in the hope that one day I shall be foolish enough to give way to you?

Can you honestly deny that that has not been your aim?'

Marcus said, and it pained him to do so. 'You have asked me to be honest, and so I shall be. Yes, in the beginning, after you had first refused me, I had that in mind, but the more I knew you the more it became impossible for me to commit such an act of betrayal. What is more, when I have told you what Jackson has discovered I shall ask you a question which will prove my honesty to you.'

Louise was in a quandary. She dearly wished to know what Jackson had found, and that being so she could not treat the bringer of that news with the contempt and dismissal which she would have done had Marcus come empty-handed. After all, it was he who had spoken to Jackson of her story, and paid him to look for the truth and the proof of it. Even if, at first, she had not wished him to do so, now that he had, and the quest was ended, she must know that truth, for good or ill, and judging by Marcus's manner, it did not seem for ill.

'Very well,' she said, 'because I half-believe you, and because you have done me a great favour you may sit there—' and she pointed at the armchair which he always used '—and you may tell me what Jackson has found.'

All the eagerness which Marcus had felt until Louise had walked into the room came surging back.

'Oh, my dear girl,' he said. 'He has returned with absolute and positive proof that Madame Félice is undoubtedly Louise Cleeve, the grand-daughter of the previous Earl of Yardley. What's more the proof, is so complete and authentic that no one could call it false or forged. With your permission we shall hand it over, once you have inspected it, to the Cleeve family lawyers so that you may return to your proper station in society.'

For the first time in her life Louise thought that she was about to faint.

'Proof? Absolute proof,' she half-whispered, 'after all this time? Where did he find it? My guardian could not. Where was it?'

Marcus told her the story which Jackson had told him, ending with the information that Sywell and Burneck had always known who she was.

At this point Louise, who was recovering herself rapidly, said, 'So *that* was why he married me. Oh, the devil, the wicked devil that he was.'

'Yes,' said Marcus, marvelling again at his love's quick wits. 'So Burneck said. Apparently they thought it a joke, he and Sywell.'

Louise rose to her feet and began to pace the room as Marcus had done earlier. 'A joke! My life was a joke for them! All that suffering, that hard work, that loneliness, not really knowing who I was or who my relatives were, fearing that I was some abandoned bastard. And all the time they thought it was a joke.'

She remembered the long and difficult hours she had spent learning her trade, and although she did not regret them, yet the knowledge that all that tedious time she had had a place in life which had been denied her was almost more than she could bear.

Before their recent difference over his bet and the revelation of their secret meeting, Marcus would have taken her in his arms to comfort her, but under the circumstances he thought that it would be tactless, would be merely mistaken for part of his campaign to overcome her.

He must be patient, for the decision he had already made before Jackson's visit, and after a sleepless night spent pondering on it, meant that in a moment or two he would say something which meant that Louise would never have cause to doubt his honesty again.

Instead, he said, 'Shall I ring for the maid to bring you some tea—or even something stronger?' for her face was so pale and her manner so shocked that he felt that she might need some kind of sustenance.

Louise shook her head and said in a strong voice, 'No, I must not have the vapours like a fool who has never had to face the hardships of life. I am trying to believe that what you are telling me is true. It makes me look at my previous life in a totally new light. My guardian told me when he lay dying that I was Rupert Cleeve's daughter, which gave me a name, but not legitimacy, and now you have given me both, which means that I must apologise for speaking so harshly to you when you arrived.'

'Very understandable of you to feel harsh towards

me after listening to Lady Leominster,' Marcus said, moving a little closer to where she stood, her hand now on the mantelpiece to steady herself. 'I left myself open to such accusations because of my behaviour to you when we first met. Now, if you feel well enough to deal with more revelations I have a very important question to ask you.'

Did she feel well enough to answer an important question? No, but the main rule of Louise's life had been never to admit weakness, or bow to it. So why should she do so now? Besides, what else could he have to say to her which could either shock or surprise her? Louise was afterwards to wonder how naïve she had been to ask herself such a question!

So she turned and shook her head at him. Unknown to her, her colour was returning, and the man who loved her thought that she had never looked more beautiful nor more gallant. He moved even nearer to her, took her hand and said hoarsely, 'My dear, it would please me if you would sit down before I ask my question.'

Louise was still so shocked that she did not refuse him but sat down immediately, to leave him standing before her, straight and tall, looking down at her with the most tender expression on his face.

'My dear Louise,' he said, 'I am about to do something which I have never done before—and hope never to have to do again. I cannot sufficiently express the admiration which I have come to feel for you over the last few weeks, and the reservations which you expressed earlier about my behaviour have only enhanced that admiration, not dimmed it. If that were not enough, I have also come to love you dearly, something which I had never thought to do for any woman before. That being so, pray make me the happiest man in England by agreeing to become my wife.'

Marcus had not thought beforehand of what Louise's reaction to this splendid proposal might be. If he had he would have thought that after it she would fall gratefully and lovingly into his arms.

He had not only brought her a magnificent prize, her true name and her legitimacy, but he had also offered her his heartfelt love, so that when she leaped to her feet and exclaimed, 'Certainly not! I see what this is all about. When I was Madame Félice the *modiste* the only thing that I was fit for was to be your mistress, but, of course, Louise Cleeve, the descendant of Earls, is quite a different thing. *She* must be your wife. If Mr Marks had offered for Madame Félice, without knowing that she was either the Honourable Louise Cleeve, or the Marchioness of Sywell, then *that* would have been a different thing and would have earned him a yes immediately. But as it is, my answer must be a most definite No.'

Marcus was thunderstruck. He did something completely out of character. He fell on his knees before her to plead with her, and took her hand in his—but she rejected it, and threw it from her, her face stony.

'No!' he exclaimed. 'You wrong me. I had already made up my mind to marry you before Jackson discovered your true identity, but I wanted to tell you of it and offer for you at the same time.'

'So you say now,' said Louise, the tears not far away. All her life everything important which had happened to her had turned to dross, and now even Marcus's proposal seemed to be tainted because he had never offered her marriage before he had discovered that she was Louise Cleeve, but only after. 'So you say now.'

Marcus was suddenly desperate. 'Only consider,' he begged of her. 'Ever since we first met we have each been drawn to the other, otherwise you would never have allowed me to become your friend—you would have rejected me immediately. I know that I was attracted to you the moment I saw you. Say yes, my darling, only say yes.'

But she turned her head away from him again, saying, 'I was lonely. You lightened my loneliness, that was all.'

'No.' And now he rose and moved towards her, to try to take again the hand which she had pulled away from him after he had made his proposal, but still she refused him.

It was hopeless—for the moment at least. He remembered the old adage: He who fights and runs away will live to fight another day. He would leave now, not torment her, but he would return, for he could not lose her now, he could not. More than ever he wanted to make her his wife, not only because he loved and desired her, but because he wished her to be the mother of his children.

Even the stoic spirit which she was displaying while refusing him had only served to make him love her the more. Her strength of will, her determination to be true to herself, impressed a man who valued such attributes almost before anything else. Perhaps, when he had gone and she had had time to consider carefully everything which he had told her, she might change her stubborn mind.

After all, she had received so many great shocks recently that it would only be when she had recovered from them that she could contemplate his proposal objectively, and realise that the strength of his passion lay behind it.

If he deluded himself, then so be it—but he must not trouble her now.

He rose to his feet and said as calmly as he could, 'I will leave you to think over all that I have said today, and hope that when you have done so you might feel able to give me a better answer.'

Louise nodded mutely, before saying, 'There is one thing which I must ask you, Lord Angmering, and I hope that of your goodness you will obey me in this. Pray bring me my mother's marriage lines and the other papers which relate to my birth. Do not give them into the keeping of lawyers before I have had time to decide what best I should do now that I know my new station in life. I may, or may not, wish to remain simple Madame Félice, for I shall never call myself the Marchioness of Sywell despite my marriage to him, and I trust that you will allow me to make that decision for myself after— as you say—due consideration. I must also ask you to say nothing to anyone of what Jackson has discovered until I have made that decision.'

'Yes,' he said simply, 'the decision must be yours. I shall see that you receive them. Only remember that you have now acquired a whole new family, who, I am sure, would wish to try to recompense you for the years of hardship which you have endured in obscurity. Their love and friendship awaits you.'

He did not say that he would bring the papers in person, for he did not wish to behave in such a manner that she might think that he was blackmailing her into receiving him when, for the moment, she had rather not.

After he had gone, closing the door carefully behind him, Louise rose and walked to the window to watch Mr Marks walk away. Since their recent friendship she still had great difficulty in thinking of Marcus as Lord Angmering. The man who wore clerk's clothing, ate oysters in the street, and talked to her so simply and cheerfully was quite unlike the few great men she had ever met.

She was not to know that the workers on the

Yardley estates in the north also thought the same of the man who walked among them wearing country clothing, who had learned how to shoe a horse, to work in the blacksmith's forge and who had insisted on being taught how to plough a straight furrow.

Some had despised him for trying to acquire the basic knowledge of a working farmer rather than sit back in his grand house and idly accept the rents which the land brought him. Some respected him because he wanted to share in their hard lives a little. Others, like Louise, were somewhat baffled by him.

But why should she be baffled? Marcus's nature was a straightforward one. He had told her quite plainly when she had first met him that he wished to make her his mistress. He had not wooed her with fair words, pretending that he was courting her, using that as the means to an end, and that end seduction, betrayal and desertion.

He had treated her more kindly than any other man she had ever met. She thought of Sywell, of the brutality which he had inflicted on her, and which had caused her to run away and hide herself from him in London—a place he detested and avoided. There had been other men whom she had met when she had visited great houses in London in order to outfit their wives, daughters and sisters. Men who had not hesitated to accost her and whisper their base desires into her ears.

There had even been one who had tricked her into

being alone with him on the pretext that his sister, for whom she was making a wedding dress, had asked that Louise visit her in her drawing-room. She had escaped ravishment only by the merest chance, and her own cunning, but the memory could still make her shiver.

No, Marcus was not like that at all, and his last words to her, that she would be acquiring a family, had struck a chord which vibrated inside her long after he had gone.

She had always been alone. The few people she had known and loved in childhood had, one by one, disappeared. Mrs Hanslope, whom she had called mother, then John, her guardian, and she had lost Athene Filmer when she had left Steepwood to be apprenticed in Northampton.

She had made few friends in London, and knowing and loving Marcus had been to her like manna found in the desert by the starving Israelites. Only her own deep sense of integrity had prevented her from consenting to be his mistress when her mind, as well as her senses, told her to accept him, if only to fill her empty world.

Louise told herself briskly not to repine. She had work to do, decisions to make, and so many different futures had opened before her—who until now, had had none—that she was quite bewildered.

Besides, she was already beginning to regret having sent Marcus away…

Chapter Seven

Marcus arrived back at Berkeley Square determined not to let the afternoon's events overset him. He cursed his own folly in not grasping what Louise's reaction to his delayed proposal of marriage would inevitably be. He was sure that her own common-sense would guide her once the shock of his news had worn off. Her unexpected refusal had only served to increase his determination to make her his wife. Nevertheless he knew that he was doomed to a few uncomfortable days, but he had survived them before.

He met his father in the entrance hall. He immediately thought that Marissa was right to worry about him: he looked old and ill.

Impulsively he said, 'Is it possible that I could have a word with you, sir? If it is convenient, that is,' for he saw his father flinch away from him a little, which disappointed him, since he had thought that they had reached a better understanding of each other since their recent confidential talk.

'Of course, Angmering, let us go to my study. While we are on our way allow me to inform you that I was buttonholed today by some fellow from the Home Office who told me that the enquiry into Sywell's death has been abandoned. Other more urgent problems relative to the state of the country—the Luddite riots in the Midland counties in particular—demand the attention of those who have been pursuing it. It seems that it must remain a mystery which might solve itself in time.'

So Jackson's task was over. He would doubtless be returning to the Midlands, but for a different reason.

'At least they will not be troubling you again, sir,' he offered as his father pointed him to a chair facing his desk.

He sat down and hesitated for a moment, not quite sure how to broach his, and Marissa's, worries to the man opposite to him. He took so long that his father said suddenly, 'Well, what is it, Angmering?'

'It's this, sir. Both Marissa and I fear that something is worrying you so much that you are beginning to look quite ill. She fears that it may be more than your health, and I share those fears. If it is possible for you to confide in me, pray do so. A trouble shared is a trouble halved. If anything is wrong it may ease matters if you speak to me of it.'

'I know,' said his father, turning his face away

from him. 'I cannot speak of it to Marissa, although she has begged me time and again to tell her what is wrong. Is it possible that I can confide in you?'

'That, sir, you must decide. Believe me, my one intent is to serve you as a good son ought, and I fear that of recent years, I have not always been the kind of son in whom you could confide—now that matters have changed perhaps you may be able to do so.'

'True, Angmering, true. For my part I have never given you credit for being the sound fellow that you are; that being so, I feel that I may trust you to hear what I have to say. At the end I would appreciate it if you would give me some notion of what you think I ought to do. It is a long story I have to tell, and not a pretty one. It goes back many years, and I fear that, at the end, you may not wish to know the man who tells it to you.'

Marcus had already heard one story which reached back in time, and now it seemed that he was to hear another. He had helped Louise, and now, strange though it seemed, his father now needed his help and advice as well.

'Until you tell me all, Father,' he said, dropping the impersonal sir, for he thought that his father looked even more ill when he had finished speaking than he had done before, 'I cannot advise you.'

'Before I begin,' his father said, 'I must ask you to treat what I shall tell you in complete confidence. You are to inform no one of it, no one, however much you think that you ought to do so. Without that assurance given to me on your word of honour, I shall say no more.'

Marcus was about to reply without thinking, 'Of course, sir. You must know that my word is my bond,' when he remembered that he had said something similar to Louise—and then he had immediately broken that word solemnly given.

One result of that betrayal—even though it had been done with the best of intentions, had inevitably been to weaken Louise's trust in him, and had probably influenced her subsequent refusal of his offer of marriage.

This time, and always in the future, whatever the cost, he would keep his word. He saw that his father, registering his hesitation, and unaware of what was causing it, had put his head in his hands as though he could no longer bear its weight.

Marcus said, and his voice rang with truth, 'You may depend upon it, father, I shall reveal nothing of whatever you are about to tell me. I will swear an oath before you to that effect if that would reassure you.'

His father lifted his head again, 'No need, no need, Angmering, your word will suffice. After all, I have little time to live, although I hope to survive long enough to see Sophia married at Christmas, and when I am gone—what I shall tell you will fall into the vast pit of the past.

'I must no longer delay. My story begins long ago

in the last century when I was even younger than you are now—when I was plain Thomas Cleeve with apparently no hope of succeeding to the Earldom since the senior and junior branches of the family had separated so long ago. It was the year 1765, and I had met a beautiful and devoutly religious young woman by the name of Sophia Goode and fallen desperately in love with her.'

He smiled a little wryly at Marcus's slight start of surprise. 'I think that you will shortly guess where your half-sister's name came from. It was I who chose it, you see, but I must resume. We were so in love that we decided to marry, since there was nothing to prevent us. Her parents and mine were delighted that we should do so, since love matches are rare in our class.

'We were about to prepare for the wedding when she sent me a letter which destroyed the happy world in which I had been living. She said that she had changed her mind about marrying me and had decided to convert to the Catholic faith. Her one wish now was not to be my bride, but to be the bride of Christ, and to achieve that end she was entering a convent.

'You may judge of the shock I sustained on reading this. I drove to her home to try to persuade her to change her mind, but she had already left and I was never to see her again in this life. I was like a madman when I realised that she had gone for ever. I railed against God and fate, since everything I saw was hateful to me if I could not see and share it with my lost love. I left for India to get away from everything which reminded me of her. After ten years I married your mother, as much from loneliness as anything else—and I was rewarded for my careless folly by the marriage being a disaster.

'Finally she left me for another, and shortly afterwards died. I was never quite sure of the circumstances, nor did I care enough about her to discover them. I was happy to be a free man again, with a son whom I wickedly neglected because he reminded me of her. Then I met Marissa, who has become my guiding star—and yours, too, a little, I think, and have been happier than perhaps I have ever deserved to be. So much time had passed that I began to forget my first love, and enjoy what was left of my life on earth without that shadow hanging over me.

'Alas, early this year I received a package which contained a few small personal possessions and a letter which was addressed to me. It came from someone called Sister Mary Margaret, something which puzzled me until I read it. It told me, among other things, that she was my dear, lost love. The package had been sent to me by the Abbess of her convent because she had recently died, and her last wish had been that I should receive it.

'It was bad enough to learn of her death, but what was even more shocking was what the letter told me. It explained why she had deserted me so suddenly

and without warning. She had been deliberately seduced and virtually raped by my friend, Lord
George Ormiston, he who later became the Marquis
of Sywell. Sywell was then a most attractive and
handsome man. He had traded upon her innocence,
which had been so great that she had assumed that
once having bedded her he would marry her. That
would have compelled her to give me up—but, in
any case, she no longer wished to marry me after
giving way to Sywell.

'She was grossly mistaken in him. Sywell treated
the whole business as a joke, jeered at her for expecting marriage, and she was left having betrayed
herself, myself, and the religion which she prized,
for the love of a wretch who had taken her virginity
and had then made a mock of her. She felt that she
was so damaged by what had happened that not only
could she not marry me, having dishonoured herself,
but she must retire from the world altogether.

'You may imagine my feelings after I had read
the letter. A past I had thought long dead had sprung
from the grave to revive all the misery of my departed youth. On learning of Sywell's wickedness
all that I wished for was to be revenged upon the
monster who had caused my love to leave the world
altogether. I remembered with pain the years of misery I had endured after she had gone. I burned to
see him, to reproach him…to do…I knew not what.
I forgot my happy life with Marissa in remembering

the suffering which Sywell had inflicted on the woman whom I had loved so dearly.

'I went at once to the Abbey to confront him, to reproach him, to make him pay for what he had done to me and to her. You may imagine with what results. Debauched and degenerate, he was a caricature of the man whom he had once been. He mocked me for having lost my love first to him, and then to God. He told me, laughing, ''The bitch wanted it, and it's not my fault that she had a religious fit after I'd bedded her. It seems to me you were well rid of such a silly cow. When all's said and done I did you a favour.''

'I would have killed him there and then, except that his by-blow, Burneck, was always in attendance on him, and stood by, watching him. I made up my mind to finish him off in such a fashion that no one could be suspected—even that vile brute, Burneck. So I swallowed my hate, thanked Sywell for doing me a favour, which made Burneck laugh, and even pretended to do a little business with them.

'That made it possible for me to invite Burneck to Jaffrey House on the night I had decided that I would kill Sywell. There was no moon, and no one would be likely to see me. I contrived some excuse in order to keep him at the house overnight. He slept in the servants' quarters, which meant that suspicion could not fall on him. Unfortunately, what I had not considered was that it might fall on the missing wife, Hanslope's daughter. Later, though, Jackson assured me that there was no way in which she could have committed the crime, seeing that she lived in London and had not the means to pay anyone to kill him for her.

'I dressed myself in gamekeeper's clothes in case anyone saw me in the dark. I took my pistol with me and all the way to the Abbey I thought of killing him without feeling the slightest remorse. I told myself that, for all his many crimes, he deserved to die a hateful death. I was still thinking this when I entered the Abbey and climbed up one of its secret ways so that if by ill chance anyone were about I might not be seen.

'I found Sywell in his bedroom. He was even more disgusting than when I had first confronted him over his debauchery of my love. I could not help remembering what he had been like when we were young men together: he had been a very Adonis. And now he was this wretched, bloated *thing* on the bed. He had been trying to shave his hairy face and his razor and towel lay on a table by the bed.

'He stared at me, and said blearily, ''What the hell are you doing here at this time of night, Yardley?''

'''Come to send you to hell,'' I told him. ''The ball I shall kill you with is my present to you from Sophia.'' I lifted the pistol and pointed it at the *thing*. It wasn't a man any more.

'He slipped out of bed and stood facing me. He

grunted, ''You haven't the guts, Tozzy, to kill your old friend in cold blood.''

'He had used my nickname, the one I had been given at school, and whether it was that, or something else, I don't, and shall never, know. It was as though I'd had a blinding revelation, or else my happy life with Marissa flashed before my eyes, but whatever it was, I knew that I could not kill him, even if he deserved it. I thought of what might happen if the law caught me, and of what that would do to Marissa, to *my* Sophia, and to her marriage already arranged for Christmas, by which time if I had been arrested I should be due to hang.

'It came upon me that he wasn't worth it. That he was already in hell, in a hell of his own making. By his own actions he had destroyed his beauty and addled his brains, while I, one of his victims, had survived to build myself a happy and prosperous life, and raise a loving family.

'That took a long time to say, but no time at all to think. I lowered the pistol and, like a fool, laid it on an occasional table, saying, ''Die in your own ordure, Sywell. I've no wish to put you out of your misery.''

'Oh, I had misjudged him again! He gave a great bellow and sprang at me before I could pick up the pistol. He had snatched his cut-throat razor up and was upon me in an instant, determined to kill me, whatever the ultimate cost to him. But he had misjudged his last victim. Old and feeble though I was—and am—I was infinitely more powerful than the *thing* he had become. I caught him by the wrist and wrenched the razor from his grasp, only to have him spit in my face and say, ''I told you that you hadn't the guts to kill me, Tozzy, didn't I?''

'I don't know what came over me then. It was something like the old berserker rages our Viking ancestors used to experience. I was suddenly a madman, cutting and thrusting at him until exhaustion overcame me, and he lay on the floor, dead. This time *he* was the victim of his last insult. I reeled away, throwing down the razor and picking up the pistol which had fallen to the floor. I was covered in blood myself and had to get away.

'I don't clearly remember what happened next because I was both shocked by what I had done, and at the same time could feel no remorse for having done it. After all, if I had not killed him, he would have killed me. Before I left I took Sywell's great-coat from where it had been flung on the floor and carried it away with me.

'When I reached the pool where he and I had swum as boys I stripped off my outer garments, which were soaked with his blood, and buried them—where I have no notion—I was in no condition to trouble about such things. I then washed myself, put on Sywell's coat to make me at least a little respectable, and made my way home. I met no one and reached my bedroom without disturbing anyone—so far as my valet and staff were concerned they had seen me to bed at the usual time.

'When the uproar about Sywell's murder began they were able to testify, quite truthfully, that they had seen me to my bed at the usual time, and that I was in it early the next morning. Jackson questioned me, but could not shake me. My one worry was that someone innocent might be accused of Sywell's murder—which was not a murder, but self-defence—and I would then have to confess to what I had done. I could not let another go to the gallows in my place.

'Today, as I told you earlier, I learned that the authorities believe that it is not possible either to find, or to convict, anyone of the murder. Unless something further is discovered which might reveal who killed Sywell, the matter will remain forever a mystery. All the obvious suspects, including myself, have unbreakable alibis, so the problem remains on the table, as it were.

'I have lived with this burden of knowledge on me for so long, that, coupled with the illness which my doctors believe will kill me before a year has passed, my life has become not worth living. I tell you of it in case any innocent person should be accused of murder after I am dead and gone. Then, and only then, will you take this paper which I will give you now, and which contains my confession, and hand it to the authorities—I wish no one else to suffer for what I did.'

By now the Earl's face was ashen. There was a glass of water on his desk. He drank it down with a shaking hand and looked into his son's face, which was as white as his own.

Marcus, an expression of enormous pity on his face, said, 'Of course, I will do as you ask, Father. Knowing Sywell's reputation and yours, I believe that what you did, you did in self-defence, but without witnesses you would have difficulty in proving that. More particularly because, by your own confession, you went there intending to kill him. And I quite understand what drove you to that.'

His father said, 'Thank you, Angmering. I think that I went a little mad after reading Sophia's letter. Only when I looked down at what I had done to Sywell did sanity have me in its grip again. I knew, too, that whatever else, my lost Sophia would not have wished me to seek to avenge her. Nothing excuses what I did, nor the lies I have told. I, who have always prided myself on my truthfulness, have had to live with the knowledge of my falsity…'

Marcus rose, and walked round the desk, saying, 'Stop, Father, stop! What's done is done, and besides Sywell, who got what he deserved, the only person to suffer has been yourself. In the end everything against any other suspects fell down because, fortunately, they could prove their own unshakeable innocence. Now that you have confessed, try to find peace again. Rest assured that I shall say and do nothing other than the two things which you have asked of me—silence and the passing of your confession to the authorities, if that proves to be necessary. Now, go to your room and try to rest.'

His father said simply, 'I don't deserve you, Angmering, nor do I deserve Marissa. For a time in my youth I was nearly as profligate as Sywell. Whether Sophia would have steadied me I shall never know. Only her desertion of me achieved that. Oh, God, one always thinks that the past is over and done with, but heaven help me, it returned to destroy me again.'

What could he say which would lessen his father's agony? Nothing, only gently help him to his feet, saying, 'Let me take you upstairs, father, where you may lie down and try to forget the past in sleep. Living or dead, Sywell is not worth tormenting yourself to your own death. Think that he brought his own upon him by his wickedness, and leave it at that.'

His father consented to do what his son wished and, arm in arm, the Earl of Yardley and the son whose worth he had come to value in his old age mounted the stairs together, where Thomas Cleeve, purged by his confession, at last found in sleep the peace which had long been eluding him.

Between his thwarted love for Louise and what his father had told him, Marcus was in a ferment, and that night, having helped his father to rest, was unable to sleep himself.

When at last he did he was haunted in his dreams by the terrible tale which his father had told him. Sywell rose from the dead to haunt him, and Louise was there, too, her face white with misery as it had been when she had told him her sad story.

Except that at the end, the darkness which had surrounded him lifted, and he was at Steepwood, walking in the woods, and Louise was by his side, and when he turned to look at her, her face was rosy, and her eyes were filled with love and happiness. She was carrying a bouquet of winter flowers, and was saying to him, 'There, I wish to go there…'

He tried to speak to her, but in the doing the dream vanished and he was awake in the grey light of early dawn. But the shadow which had hung over him since he had heard his father's confession had lifted, and he was ready to face the day and the future.

Louise was tired of the knowing stares which she was receiving from some of her customers these days. They told her that they had heard the gossip linking her with Marcus. Oh, nothing was said openly, but it was plain that it was going the rounds of society and would continue to do so until some new piece of scandal arose to entertain those whose lives were so dull and empty that only the current tittle-tattle could enliven them.

She had just completed the trying on of the wedding dress of yet another young woman who was to marry at Christmas, and was sitting down alone in her little office for the first time that day, when the girl who kept the shop came in, saying breathlessly, 'Oh, Madame Félice, the gentleman who wanted you to make him a shirt is here again. He said, ''Tell Madame that Mr Marks wishes to see her urgently on a matter of business.'''

Marcus! It was Marcus, calling on her in Bond Street regardless of who might see him. Whatever could he want? What was urgent? At their last meeting he had seemed to say that he would send her the documents which Jackson had recovered from Burneck—but did his presence here mean that he had changed his mind?

Her assistant, still breathless—and was that just Marcus who made her so, or was it her usual habit and she had never noticed?—said, 'What shall I tell him, mam?'

'Madame Félice, not mam,' said Louise automatically. 'Tell him that I will see him.'

And when she did what would she say then? She had thought long and hard of what she ought to do. Marry Marcus—or not marry him? Make her claim to be Louise Cleeve, the present Earl of Yardley's distant cousin—or not? Try to have her marriage to Sywell annulled—or not? She had thought of that last action after Marcus had left her, since she had no wish to be known as the Marchioness of Sywell. After all, a brief examination by midwives would be enough to confirm her untouched virginity.

Once she had thought that if she could prove who she was then the decisions which would follow would be easy ones. No such thing…

Marcus's entry put an end to these musings. He was dressed in his Mr Marks' clothing and was carrying a despatch case—for her papers presumably. Why was it that when she saw him after a few days away from him he always looked particularly desirable?

Her wayward heart gave a frisky little jump when he came in, and her breathing shortened. She told her body to behave itself, but it wouldn't. The worst thing—or was it the best?—was that he did not even have to touch her to make her feel that her only rightful place was in his arms—a place which she had never really visited.

'Do sit down, Mr Marks,' she said to him as though he were a real lawyer's clerk. 'I take it that you have come to deliver my legal papers to me.'

Oh, the darling! was Marcus's internal response to that. I have only to see her to want to make her mine in the shortest time possible, and I do believe that the minx knows that and is teasing me! That must be a good sign.

'Indeed,' he replied, with an underling's bob of the head which set her smiling, and oh, what a joy to see her looking happy. 'I decided that it would be best to deliver the documents in person. That way I would know that you had received them.'

'Very thoughtful of you,' she returned graciously,

and put out a hand for them after he had extracted them carefully from the case. 'Particularly when I understood at our last meeting that you would not come yourself.'

Marcus smiled, and arranged it so that his hand touched hers at the precise moment of take-over. His reaction to that simple contact was rather like that of one of Signor Galvani's frogs when attached to a battery—all his senses jumped together.

By Louise's expression something similar was happening to her. She was becoming even more breathless than her little assistant. She began to put the papers down, but he said immediately, 'I think that you ought to check them against the list I have made. I have also your mother's diary to give you.' And he lifted that from the case and handed that over, too, again contriving to touch her hand.

This time Louise jumped. His smile broadened, particularly when she opened the book and began to examine it. In the middle of her delight at recovering it—a delight which was in some ways even greater than that which she had felt when he had handed her the proofs of her parents' marriage and her own legitimacy—she felt a tear gather and run down her cheek, to be followed by another.

'Oh, no,' she said, dashing a hand at them, only for Marcus to pass over her desk his large linen handkerchief to help to stem the cascade which followed the preliminary two.

'I'm so sorry,' she said, 'to behave like an errant

watering-pot, particularly when you have made me so happy. But this is the only thing which I have left to me which belonged to my mother, and to have it is bitter-sweet—joy and sorrow combined.'

It was a tribute to Marcus's delicacy—something which few who knew him would have thought that he possessed—that he knew what she meant. He was sorry to see her overset, but at the same time he was pleased that her manner to him was so different from that of their last meeting.

Indeed, it was as though their last meeting, with her rejection of him, had never taken place. One further proof of their new rapprochement, and their meeting of minds, came when Louise had wiped her last tear away and they both said together, 'I have been thinking...'

They looked at one another and both of them laughed, before they both said, together again, 'You first...'

Marcus put his head on one side and adopted what Louise always thought of as his Mr Marks face— one of humble and pleasant enquiry. 'Allow me to say that after our last meeting, which was so full of disharmony, I thought that we would never be able to speak to one another again. This meeting, how-ever, is so full of harmony that—'

He paused, for Louise to say smartly, 'That we can barely speak to one another because we are too busy saying the same thing!'

'Exactly,' said Marcus. 'Why do you think that is?'

'Because,' said Louise, a trifle warily, 'I have been thinking over our situation very carefully and, among other things, I have concluded that I behaved extremely badly to you at our last meeting. You had taken a great deal of trouble to find out something which I have wanted to know all my life, and your only reward was for me to reject you in the rudest fashion possible. After that I wonder why you should ever wish to speak to me again! I decided that when, or rather if, we next met I should try to be as civil as possible to you.'

'Oh, no,' said Marcus, 'do not reproach yourself. You had a great shock and when I began to think matters over I rapidly grasped how tactless I had been to propose marriage to you at such a juncture. You see, my darling, since wearing the lawyers' clerk's clothes I am beginning to talk exactly like one of them. My hurt pride made me short with you, and altogether I made a fine mess of things. But then, I always was a bull at a gate.'

'Dear Mr Marks,' said Louise affectionately, smiling at him through a shimmer of tears, present, but refusing to fall. 'The word you should have used was we. We both made a fine mish-mash of things, did we not? I refuse to allow you to take the blame.'

'By all means, let us agree to share it,' exclaimed Marcus. 'Recently I had a conversation with my father which made me realise how short life is, and how quickly we must grasp happiness to us when we meet it, lest it fly by and be gone forever. I immediately determined that I would come to you as soon as possible and try to mend matters. It does rather seem, though, that we are of like mind, since I take it, from what you have said, that you felt exactly the same as I did.'

'Indeed,' said Louise. 'But I also have to tell you that I have not yet made up my mind what to do about these…' And she waved a hand at the papers. 'There is another matter, too, which troubles me, and that is that I do not wish, ever, to be known as the Marchioness of Sywell, and I would want the marriage to be annulled—if that is possible now that he is dead. I was a fool to agree to marry him, but my guardian was dying when he begged me to accept Sywell. He had been so kind to me that I did not wish to distress him by refusing his last wishes. Nor did I then know how great a monster Sywell was. I wish to be rid of him, once and for all.'

'Well,' said Marcus, 'my advice is that you go to a genuine lawyer, and not the false one I am, and talk to them about the legal implications of your papers and whether or not you may petition for an annulment. I must say that I have no wish to marry the Marchioness of Sywell, even if Louise Cleeve agrees to my proposal. But I see by your expression that you have not made up your mind about that.'

'No.' Louise was restless.

She rose from her chair and walked to a small

side-table which held a jug of water and a pair of matching glasses. More so that she could recover herself a little and decide what she had to say in a manner which would not cause Marcus further hurt, than for any other reason, she said, 'I need a drink of water. Would you care for a glass, too?'

'Yes,' said Marcus, who understood that this delaying tactic meant that Louise was probably about to tell him something which he did not wish to hear. 'Talking is thirsty work, and I am not used to it. The farmers and artisans I deal with on father's northern estates are silent creatures. We converse in monosyllables.'

'And we have scarcely been doing that,' agreed Louise, handing him his glass. 'I hope that you will understand that what I am about to tell you is not my final word. The truth is that I am torn in two. You see, I am building up a fine business here in Bond Street and if I were to marry you then I should have to give it up. The wife of Yardley's heir cannot be a tradeswoman entering the homes of his friends as something little more than a servant when she is engaged on business there. On the other hand—' and she paused to take a sip of her so far neglected drink '—on the other hand I find that I am in love with Yardley's heir and would wish to be his wife. I trust that you see my dilemma.'

She had not yet sat down at her desk again, but stood before him having laid her glass upon it.

Marcus, his face ablaze, rose, and before she

could stop him, took her in his arms. 'You love me! That is all I know—and all I need to know. Oh, my darling heart, I have longed to hear you say these words. I have confessed my love to you, but I had no notion whether or not it was returned. Oh, to hell with words, they are not my *métier,* not my *métier* at all. This I do know—and it is better than any words.' And he began to kiss her passionately, his right hand holding her head, his left around her shoulders, so that his kisses might rove around her face like butterflies softly alighting.

He was, at first, gentle with her, for he knew her to be a virgin, and a virgin who might have been ill-treated by that swine, Sywell. At first she resisted him a little, but then her passion, fuelled by his, grew to the point where they were exchanging kiss for kiss and caress for caress until they were both so aroused that they neither knew nor cared what they were doing on the inevitable path to consummation.

Louise had never before experienced the sensations which were sweeping over her. For the first time she understood the power of the passion which could overwhelm a man and a woman: a passion which was heedless of propriety, of circumstance, of the social differences between them. So fiercely was she affected that her response to him surprised her.

They remained, twined together, lost to the world, until Marcus, the more experienced of the two, broke away from her, gasping, 'Not here, not now, anyone might enter and find us. I must not ruin you when you have not yet accepted my offer of marriage. You will accept it, won't you? Say that you will.'

Louise, her hair dishevelled, her eyes dilated, her lips swollen, and her face rosy from their recent passion, at last managed to offer him a coherent answer.

'I may not do so until I have solved my two conundrums—whether I wish to become Louise Cleeve, or whether I wish to remain Madame Félice. Oh,' she suddenly wailed, 'what shall I do, Marcus?' For since he had taken her in his arms and begun to make love to her, he was no longer either Lord Angmering, or simple Mr Marks, but only Marcus. Marcus who loved her. Marcus whom she now knew that she loved.

'I am being unfair to you,' she ended sadly. 'I know I am.'

'Unfair to both of us,' he whispered, still standing away from her, since he dare not touch her lest they both go up in flames again. 'Do not be long before you make a decision, I beg of you.'

'By Saturday,' she said. 'Visit me again on Saturday—as Lord Angmering this time. I am sick of shams. I have unknowingly lived a lie all my life, and do not wish to tell any more, either knowingly, or unknowingly.'

Marcus nodded agreement, even though the four days which would pass before Saturday arrived would seem an eternity.

It was only after he had gone, with one last agonised look at her, that Louise knew that, when she had told him to call on her as Lord Angmering, she had already—unknowingly—made her decision.

It only remained to inform him of it.

Chapter Eight

On his way home, for he had come to think of
Berkeley Square as home, Marcus was accosted by
none other than Jackson. If the Runner thought that
M'lord was a little oddly dressed, nothing in his
manner betrayed it to Marcus. Marcus, for his part,
was too busy going over in his mind his recent en-
counter with Louise to trouble about such trifles as
his clothing.

'A word with you, m'lord, if you would allow me
the liberty of speaking to you in the street.'

'Certainly,' said Marcus. 'As you see, I am
dressed for such an occasion. No one will remark
upon us.'

'Quite so, m'lord—or should I call you Mr
Marks?'

Marcus could not help laughing. He clapped the
Runner on the shoulder, exclaiming, 'Is nothing hidden from you, man? Have you been tracking the
man who employed you to track others? If so I can

only commend you for your diligence—and your impudence. I cannot decide which is the greater.'

'Quite, so,' said Jackson with a grin. 'The more a thief-taker knows, the better he is at his chosen task. I have been keeping a weather eye on Madame F—which meant keeping one on you when you decided to visit her. Her little maid was very helpful. She told me when I took her to the fair that you were Madame's cousin—which, of course, is true— and a lawyer's clerk, which isn't. Now I no longer need to keep an eye on either of you. I suppose that your pa told you that my masters have decided to end the enquiry into Sywell's murder?'

'He did, indeed. Which leads me to wonder why you should feel a need to speak to me.'

'Well, m'lord, it's like this. One might think one knows who did commit the foul deed—if murdering the likes of Sywell can be called foul—but it's a different matter to prove it in a court of law. Convincing evidence is sadly lacking—all the possible principals having splendid alibis—including your pa, which let him off the hook. To be honest he was my prime suspect; he had a lot to avenge, what with his family losing the Abbey and all—but pinning him down might be difficult. Besides, my masters wouldn't like me to go around accusing belted Earls of murder without proof.'

He stopped and gave Marcus what could only be described as a meaningful leer. 'Now, you're a right sharp fellow—not in the least like most of the nobility and gentry I've had to deal with. Follow the plough and shoe the horse, eh? Now, if you'd not been in Northumbria when the deed was done, you'd have topped my list of suspects, but you had the best alibi of the lot—'

'I didn't know that I either needed one, or had one,' said Marcus with a grin as knowing as Jackson's.

'Aye, but like father, like son, I always say. Now, take your pa. Went to India and made a fortune didn't he? By his own efforts, and not many of the nobs do that. He's a man what does things, what looks after his own. A man I can respect, not a swine like Sywell. So then I ask myself, what's justice? Sure as fate, it ain't the law—or leastways, not always. I'm sure you takes my meaning. So, I tells my masters that, to my regret, I have no proof of who might have topped Sywell. I didn't say, after all I had heard about the swine, that whoever did it should be given a medal—except that he didn't finish the job properly, and do for that slimy devil Burneck as well. Now, *his* alibi interested me the most, particularly when I knew who had arranged it. Enough said, eh?'

'If I knew what you were trying to tell me, Jackson, I might agree with you.'

'Oh, but you do, m'lord, don't you? Now you may both sleep easy—for your different reasons acourse. I wish you well—though by the looks of him your pa ain't long got much longer on this earth.

Let's hope Heaven's law—or justice, call it what
you will, is better than ours. Who's to say?'

He gave Marcus one last bow, sweeping off his
greasy hat with an 'I bid you good day, m'lord,' and
was off, crossing the road, where he was soon lost
to view among the passing crowds.

He knows, thought Marcus dazedly, he knows,
and he has, in his own words, let my father 'off the
hook'. How the devil does he know?

Which was a question Marcus was never able to
answer to his own satisfaction. What he *did* know
was, that for his own reasons, Jackson had spared
his father obloquy and the hangman's noose.

Still another confrontation awaited him when he
entered Cleeve House. His father and stepmother
met him before he had mounted the main staircase
to go to his room to change into something more
fitting for the Earl of Yardley's heir.

They both stared at him. His father said, more
mildly than he would have done a few weeks ago,
'What the devil are you doing in that get-up,
Angmering? Bit early in the day for a masquerade,
isn't it?'

Thinking furiously on his feet, Marcus said cheerfully, 'I've been working with a friend's horse this
morning, and I'm about to change.'

'Really, Angmering? Really?' said the Earl. 'If
that was so, why are you not wearing something
more suitable than a clerk's clothing? I thought you

were one of Lawyer Herriott's men come to badger me about my will. Which reminds me, I would wish to speak to you this afternoon about some of the minor details. You know the major ones so far as they affect you already.'

'Certainly, father,' Marcus replied, stifling a grin at his father's cheerful sarcasm about his clothes. 'When I am more suitably in the pink, perhaps, than I am now. Or would a clerk's clothing be more suitable for examining a clerk's work than appearing dressed as a member of the dandy set?'

Marissa who had also been smiling at this agreeable exchange of rudenesses, added her own contribution to them. 'My dear Marcus, however finely you dress you never look remotely like a member of the dandy set. Everything about you is too down-to-earth for that.'

'Oh,' said Marcus, pulling a comic face, 'I can see how much of a disappointment I am to you both.'

'Indeed, not,' said Marissa, leaning forward to re-tie his well-worn linen cravat for him. 'I much prefer your down-to-earth manner to the false and artificial compliments and dress for which the dandy set are famous. The only thing is, I would dearly like to know the reason for your present appearance. I hope the explanation does you credit, that's all.'

'Very much so, dear Mama.' And Marcus gave his stepmother a kiss on her cheek. 'When I ultimately tell you the reason for it, you will quite understand and forgive me.'

With that he bounded upstairs to change into clothing more suitable for Yardley's heir. Its only drawback was that it was so much less comfortable than his clerk's humble attire. Nevertheless when he walked into his father's study to discuss the draft of the will which a true lawyer's clerk had left with him, the Earl looked approvingly at him, saying, 'I wish you would always take such care of yourself, Angmering.'

He received in reply another cheerful smile from Marcus, and: 'Exactly what my valet has just said to me, sir. Depend upon it, I will try to follow your joint advice in future.'

Even his father, usually so staid and proper, laughed at that piece of impudence.

'And now,' he said, 'let us get down to work. I informed you the other day of the main thrust of the will so far as it affects you, Marissa and the Neds. I do however, have one problem, and that relates to our cousin Rupert's lost daughter. The estate and its moneys came to me as the next Earl, unencumbered by any dower or provision for his child. I feel, though, that it is my duty to make some kind of reference to her in my will when all the other settlements are finalised.'

Marcus was in a quandary. He wanted to tell his father that Lord Rupert's daughter was no longer lost, and more than that, that he wished to marry her! But he had given his word to Louise to say nothing about her having the power to prove that she was the missing Cleeve daughter until she had decided whether to claim her birthright. Since he had once nearly lost her love because he had broken his word, he was of no mind to do it again—and lose her for good.

He sat silent for a moment before saying, 'I honour you, sir, for wishing to remember her, which was more than her father was able to do. Perhaps you could put in trust a sum large enough to give her a useful income if, by chance, she were ever found. Something in the order of what her father would have left her, had he been spared to return to England.'

'Excellent, Angmering,' said his father energetically. 'I was thinking of something along those lines. I will see to it immediately. Now there are a number of other, more minor matters we must discuss before Marissa summons us to partake of this newfangled notion, tea in the afternoon!'

Marcus nodded and they worked until Cardew threw the door open and announced, 'Tea is served in the blue drawing-room, m'lords.'

If Saturday could not come soon enough for Marcus, Louise was in the same case. One thing which he had said affected her more powerfully every time she thought of it: that she would be gaining a real family, something which she had never possessed before.

Sometimes this thought frightened her. She had already met Lady Yardley and Lady Sophia, and they both seemed to be good and kind—they had always treated her considerately—unlike some other great ladies. But what would they think, and how would they behave when a nobody of a *modiste* entered their lives claiming to be their cousin? How would society and the ton treat her then?

Her reappearance would, of course, create the most intense excitement. Some would not believe that she was Louise Cleeve, even though not only the documents which she possessed, but also her appearance, would give the lie to such doubts. Was it perhaps even possible that Marcus's reputation might be harmed if he married her?

Fortunately at this point her sense of humour, and her common-sense, took over. One thing was sure, Marcus would not give a damn about what others thought of him, or his reputation—so no need to trouble herself about *that*.

Her other worry about ceasing to be Madame Félice was soon put to rest. There was no reason why she should not continue to be the business's patron. She could put in her chief sempstress, a middle-aged woman of great competence and taste, as its manager. If Lord Yardley could run his India business from England then surely, she, when Lady Angmering, could run a business in London from an infinitely shorter distance. She would always be there to offer help and advice—if any were needed.

Thus the last obstacle to her agreeing to accept Marcus's proposal of marriage being out of the way, she would tell him on Saturday that she would accept it—something which she had once thought that she would never do.

But then, she had not realised how deeply she would fall in love with him: she could not visualise a world in which she and Marcus would not live together. The ugly ghost of Sywell, her late husband, was banished into a limbo from which it would never return, and she could only thank God that he had never made her his true wife.

Saturday morning saw her dressed in her most elegant walking-out gown. It was a pale green, to enhance her porcelain complexion and her hair. Cut on classic lines, it cleared the ground so that a pair of dainty black shoes with tiny silver buckles could be seen—as well as a pair of trim ankles. Her bonnet was so small that her hair and face were not hidden by it, and the ribbon which tied it was of the same colour as the dress.

That and her reticule lay beside her on the sofa when the housekeeper—the little maid was out on an errand—came in to inform her: 'A man who calls himself Lord Angmering is at the door and asking to call on you, but, madame, I think that I ought to inform you that he is the man who has been here several times before. He was then calling himself

Mr Marks.' She stopped, but was obviously bursting to go on, so Louise said gently, 'Yes, what is it? Something is troubling you.'

'Oh, madame,' said the woman anxiously, 'I know that you run a business and seem to know what's what, but you are still only a young woman. Do not think me impertinent, and do not know my place, if I tell you that the gentry and nobility often use such tricks in order to deceive and betray women whom they are pursuing. Pray be cautious, I beg of you. He seemed a nice enough young fellow when he called himself Mr Marks, but Lord Angmering—why, he may be quite a different kettle of fish—if you will pardon me for saying so.'

Louise rose and took her by the hand. 'Do not worry, my dear,' she said. 'It is kind of you to warn me, but I have known since I first met him that his true name is Lord Angmering. He called himself Mr Marks so as not to embarrass me, and his visit to me today is an honourable one. Now please go and admit him immediately. He has been kept waiting for so long that he may be thinking that something is wrong.'

'You are not annoyed by my frankness…' the housekeeper began.

'Indeed, not. Now do as I bid.'

If Louise thought that she had dressed herself rather magnificently for Marcus's visit, she found when he entered that he completely outshone her. He was, for once, dressed like a very tulip of fash-

ion. His valet had outdone himself in his delight that
M'lord should wish to look like a proper gentleman
for once, and so he had told Marcus who had
laughed, saying, 'Oh, do I usually look like an improper one, then?'

To have his man answer severely, 'You know perfectly well what I mean, m'lord. I wish that you
always took such care. You really do repay for
dressing, if I may say so.'

'Oh, indeed you may say so,' replied Marcus.
'But do not think that you are going to get me up
like the veriest painted maypole every day. By no
means. I prefer to be comfortable. I am sure that I
shall not be able to sit down in these breeches.'

'Now you are funning, m'lord,' said his valet. 'I
told the tailor that you didn't want them skintight
and he nearly had a fit of the vapours at the notion
that they might be loose, but I hounded him until he
did my bidding. Not that that pleased me any more
than it did him.'

'I wish to God you had to wear the damned
breeches,' muttered Marcus, but he had to admit
when he saw himself in the long glass that, as his
man said again before he left, he looked ready to
rival all the beaux who decorated London society—
and what a pathetic ambition that was!

He got his reward, however, when Louise said to
him, 'No wonder that my housekeeper was overset
when she saw you. She has spent the last five
minutes warning me against such fine gentlemen as

you. She agrees wholeheartedly with the old song, ''One foot on land, one foot on sea, Men were deceivers ever.'''

'So that was why I was kept waiting on the doorstep,' exclaimed Marcus. 'I began to fear that you had changed your mind about receiving me.'

'No, I gave you my word, and I always keep it.' She looked expectantly at him. 'I assured her that your intentions were honourable. I do hope that you have not been deceiving me.'

'Not at all,' Marcus said, bowing low. 'But, for some reason, I do not wish to propose to you here. I have come in a curricle as well as in modish splendour, and I would like to drive you to somewhere romantical—I believe that is the word which ladies use—to make my proposal in the hope that it might soften your hard heart a little.'

He said this because everything about Louise's expression, added to her beautifully elegant toilette, seemed to tell him that he was about to receive a favourable answer. He hoped to God that he was going to be proved right—if only because wearing these damned clothes would not have proved a waste of time.

Or so he told himself, if only to prevent himself from being over-confident of the answer which he expected from her.

'I have never,' Louise told him, her eyes shining, 'been driven in a curricle before.'

'I guessed that, my darling girl, so I thought that

between providing you with a splendid treat, as well as allowing you to admire the River Thames from on high, I might, by doing so, be able to bend you to my wicked will—as your housekeeper might put it—except that, as you already know, my intentions are completely honourable.'

He offered her his hand, smiling and bowing, for he was sure of one thing—that if she were not prepared to accept him, Louise would not have accepted his offer of a drive in his curricle, either.

Outside the house a tiger, clad in gold and black stripes so that he resembled a large wasp, was holding the reins of two chestnuts who, he told Marcus, were rapidly growing impatient.

'Thought you was never coming out,' he grumbled, adding 'm'lord' as an afterthought.

The curricle itself was a gorgeous thing: like the tiger it was also picked out in black and gold.

'Yours?' queried Louise, entranced, when she was finally seated beside him, with the tiger up behind them—she had not associated Marcus with such a frippery thing.

'Alas, no,' he sighed. 'It belongs to a friend of mine, namely my sister's future husband, Sharnbrook, who has lent it to me with the promise that he will call me out for pistols at dawn if I do not return it to him in the same condition it was in when he handed it over. So I must ask you to behave yourself with due decorum at all times. No larking about which might disturb the horses, please, and cause an upset—not even larking of what I believe is called the genteel kind.'

Louise was growing to like it when Marcus teased her. She had never been teased—or flirted with—before. The normal life of most pretty young women had passed her by.

'I promise to behave myself,' she said demurely, 'just so long as you propose to behave yourself.'

'Now as to that,' said Marcus, preparing to negotiate a difficult corner in order to enter King's Road which, as was usual on a Saturday morning was full of traffic. 'The reason I came in the curricle was in order to propose to you in public, because were I to do so in your drawing-room, and were you to accept me, I fear that were we in private I should have a great deal of difficulty in controlling myself once you had done so! You, my darling girl, are temptation personified.'

'Really?' asked Louise. 'Really, Marcus?'

'Yes, really, and if you look at me like that again, we shall have the tiger telling me to behave myself. Tigers are the most dreadful tyrants, are they not, Jarvis?' he called over his shoulder.

'If you say so, m'lord.'

'I do say so.'

They were now running along the road towards Pimlico and Belgravia which ran parallel with the river, and where Louise was a little worried that they might be seen and recognised.

She told Marcus so.

'No need,' he said. 'We shall shortly stop and turn off on to the Embankment—you remember the Embankment?—where Jarvis will dismount and look after the horses and carriage for us. I have brought us a long way round because I wanted you to have the pleasure of the drive before I popped the question, as I believe it is called in lesser circles than ours.'

He gave a little laugh. 'What could be more romantical than proposing to you on the banks of the Thames in the middle of an Indian summer, as the Yankees call this warm autumn weather.'

Marcus is in such high spirits that he must be sure that I am going to accept him, thought Louise. I am, but how can he know that? Of course, what a nodcock I am! He knows me, and that I would not be dressed in the pink of fashion if I were going to refuse him—and here is the Embankment again, and I must think what I am going to say to him.

'This is the bench we sat on before,' said Marcus, after he had handed the curricle over to Jarvis and told him to take a short spin in it. 'You remember the occasion, I am sure. I was Mr Marks but you were still Madame Félice of unknown origin, and now I am Lord Angmering, and you are Louise Cleeve. Do you feel any different, my darling heart?'

'Oh, a little strange,' she said. 'But not much has changed yet. I am not Louise Cleeve, nor will be until the lawyers have settled matters. I went to one

the other day, a man called Herriott. I had heard
Lady Leominster talking of him. I showed him my
documents and told him that Messrs Jackson and
Burneck would testify that I was the child named in
them who was rescued by John Hanslope all those
years ago. I suppose that Mr Burneck will testify,'
she added a trifle anxiously. 'So I am afraid that we
shall have to wait a little before you can introduce
me to your family as Rupert Cleeve's long-lost
daughter.'

'Oh, yes,' said Marcus with a knowing grin. 'We
can sic Jackson on to Burneck again if he tries to
refuse. As for Herriott, he is a proper bulldog of a
fellow I am told. You chose well.'

'Yes, but it seems that since Sywell is dead I may
not have my marriage annulled because I cannot
bring a lawsuit against a dead man. What I can do,
he said, is renounce the title and call myself Louise
Cleeve when that is settled. For the moment you are
sitting beside Louise Hanslope. Apart from my business I shall not call myself Madame Félice again.'

'I don't give a damn what name you use when I
sit by you,' said Marcus determinedly, 'since I am
now about to ask you to marry me, and if you accept
me, which I beg that you will, since I am so lost in
love for you that I am beginning to fade away, you
shall be Louise Cleeve, Lady Angmering. I can't go
on my knees here—you will have to imagine that.
Good God! I am beginning to wish that I had not
been so virtuous. This would all be a deal easier if

we had stayed at your home, and I could have kissed and cuddled you to my heart's content when you did say yes.'

'As I am about to do exactly that,' said Louise putting on an expression of mock severity, 'it is probably just as well that you brought me here, since I don't think that we should have stopped at mere kissing and cuddling—and I have no wish to go to my marriage forsworn, if you take my meaning. As for fading away, I have seldom seen you look more robust!'

'I'm marrying a Puritan, and a truthful one at that,' moaned Marcus extravagantly, 'and even if we are in public I am going to give you a surreptitious kiss.' And he proceeded to do so just as Jarvis brought the curricle back.

'Well done, m'lord,' said Jarvis when Marcus helped Louise back to the curricle. 'I see that you and your lady have not been wasting your time, if I may say so.'

'No, you may not,' said Marcus, but his voice was amused. 'Does Sharnbrook allow you all this familiarity?'

Jarvis sniggered. 'Oh, he's a rare one is His Grace. He likes to know what's what, and we go a long way back, but enough said about that.' And he put his finger by his nose. 'Home again, is it?'

'Back to my lady's,' said Marcus. 'We are about to celebrate our recent betrothal by drinking a decorous dish of tea. Then you may return the curricle to your master and I will call a Hackney cab to take me home again.'

'I thought that you dared not be alone with me,' Louise twitted him when Jarvis had disappeared down the road.

'Oh, that was before, but this is after. I will try to behave myself, but I cannot guarantee that I will. Cry no, if I exceed myself, and I promise to obey you.'

'Which puts the responsibility back on to me,' sighed Louise. 'What a fine marriage we are going to have, if this is how we begin!'

'Except that we are not yet married,' Marcus pointed out as they walked into the hall.

'True, now let me order nuncheon for two and at least try to be good while we eat that.'

'Am I to understand, then,' said Marcus, offering her a wicked look, 'that after nuncheon licence may reign supreme? I will be sure to remember that when afterwards arrives.'

Oh, what a wicked tongue he had! Louise had never enjoyed herself so much before. Her early life had been a hard one, with little fun and laughter in it, but Marcus was rapidly remedying that sad situation. She had never thought that love could be so happy.

Even while they were eating their nuncheon, served by a housekeeper delighted by the news that they were to be married and that her mistress was not to be the prey of an unscrupulous nobleman,

Marcus kept up a running fire of light-hearted rail-
lery.

And afterwards? Why, afterwards he made gentle
love to her, beginning to teach her its grammar, and
nobly, at some pain to himself, refraining from taking her too far along the path towards their passion's
final consummation. His reward was her flushed,
joyful face, and after he had awakened her slum-
bering senses, her co-operation with him in the early
games of love rapidly grew and blossomed.

At last, he disengaged himself gently from her
and whispered hoarsely, 'You have not cried no, but
I must. I would have a virgin bride, even if I do not
deserve one, since my life has been as careless as
that of most young men of title. I would not mock
the wedding ceremony by anticipating it with you,
and I believe you feel the same.'

Louise offered him dazed eyes. 'I had not understood how easily one might find one's self breaking
the conventions which bind us. I have always wondered how girls could allow themselves to be seduced—but now I know. Had you chosen to go on
making love to me, I could not have resisted you,
so sweet and powerful are the feelings which are
overcoming me. Are they overcoming you?'

'Of course,' Marcus said, privately cursing his errant body which was finding consummation rejected
a painful experience. 'Which is why I stopped. Now
we must order ourselves a little and make some
plans for the future. I believe that you have agreed

that you will declare yourself a Cleeve to my family, as soon as the lawyers have acted. Once that has happened we may tell my father and the others that we are betrothed. My sister, Sophia, as you know, is being married at Christmas. I would have preferred an earlier wedding, but I think that it would give my father and Marissa a great deal of pleasure if we were to be married at the same time. Unless, of course, your memories of Steepwood are too painful for you to agree to that.'

Louise shook her head. 'Not all my memories are painful. I remember some happy times with Athene, and I would wish for her, and her husband, to be present. It will be a strange experience for me to make my own wedding dress—and not someone else's!'

'So that is settled,' said Marcus, 'and now I must leave you, lest temptation strike again. When your legitimacy is settled we shall be able to meet more easily, and on equal terms—and I cannot wait for that day.'

'Nor I,' said Louise, and after he had gone she sat and dreamed of a time when she and Marcus would not be parted, and when she would have a family of her own, a settled place in the world, and a name which was not an assumed one.

Marcus's father had intended to stay only a short time in London, but his physician had persuaded him that he should not return to the country, where medical help for his condition would not be adequate.

'Wait until we are sure that we can do nothing more for you,' he had said. 'It is possible that my diagnosis may be wrong, and if so, you may need other treatment—again of a kind you would not easily find in the Midlands.'

'If I am going to die fairly soon I would prefer to do so at Jaffrey House,' grumbled the Earl. 'London is not my favourite place on earth—it's too smelly and too dirty.'

'Nevertheless,' the man persisted. 'It will not be for long, I promise you.'

Marissa had backed him, and even Marcus when consulted had said of his father's medical adviser in his own forthright way, 'Why buy a dog and bark yourself, sir?'

'You seem uncommon cheerful these days,' his father had replied, but he had taken his son's advice.

The Earl was dozing in his study some weeks after Marcus had proposed to Louise when his son came in—looking dashed happy as usual. He had to hope that he wasn't smoking opium like some other damned fools the Earl knew. The biggest damned fool was, of course, himself, since the physician had prescribed it to ease the occasional strong pain he had begun to feel.

'Sir,' Marcus said, 'I wish to talk to you about matters of some importance. I am of the opinion that you will be both relieved, and astonished, when I have finished.'

'Eh, what's that?' said the Earl, recovering himself slowly from sleep. 'Something about your coming management of the Abbey?'

'In a sense,' Marcus said. He wanted his father to be happy, because every day he seemed to grow more transparent, more wraith-like. His illness was beginning to consume him. 'It is about two things. One is my marriage, and the other is the lady whom I intend to marry.'

'Marry!' exclaimed the Earl. 'Have you come to your senses at last? If so, I shall be ready to die happy, knowing that everything will be in competent hands, and the continuance of the line will be ensured.'

'Well, as to that only time will tell,' grinned Marcus, 'and we still have the Two Neds to fall back on. However, I not only intend to marry, but the lady has agreed that the ceremony should be celebrated at Christmas at the same time as that for Sharnbrook and Sophia—if they are agreeable, that is.'

'But will not your bride's family wish to see her married from her home?'

'Well, as to that, sir, that is the second matter of which I wish to speak. I believe that she will, after a strange fashion, be married from her home. You see, my intended bride is none other than the missing daughter of Lord Rupert Cleeve, whom Jackson and myself, acting in company, have discovered. She is also the missing widow of the late Marquis of Sywell who was supposed to be the daughter of John Hanslope, his bailiff, and was always known as Louise Hanslope.

'She has proved her identity and her legitimacy beyond a doubt, and the lawyers are satisfied that her claim is a true one. An examination by midwives has also shown her to be virgin. I had to persuade her to reveal her identity, because she originally wished to remain private and anonymous, and not cause you all distress by making such a claim. But I have convinced her that she owes a duty to herself, and to our family, to reveal her true identity. I now have her permission to speak to you of this. I must also tell you that Marissa and Sophia already know her.'

Marcus paused, for now here came the difficult part of his explanation. His father's face was a picture of bewilderment when he had said that his stepmother and half-sister knew his proposed bride.

His father filled the pause by saying, 'You mean that I do not know the lady, but they do, but how can that be?'

'Because—' and Marcus bit the bullet '—she is now known as Madame Félice, the *modiste* who is making Sophia's wedding dress and trousseau.'

'And you are marrying her—a—dressmaker! How in the world did you ever come to know her?'

'That, sir, is a long story, and not to be told now,'

said Marcus firmly. 'But she is the woman I love and whom I intend to marry. I believe that you, too, will come to love her when you meet her. I wish to bring her here as soon as possible so that I may introduce her to her family as our cousin and my future wife.'

'Well, well, Angmering,' said his father. 'I suppose that you know what you are doing, you usually do. But I do hope that the lady will not wish to continue being a dressmaker after you marry her! Sywell's widow, you say? Now that is an astonishing turn-up, you must admit.'

And that, thought Marcus with an inward grin, was rather how he might have expected his father to react to what must have seemed to him, amazing news.

What he said was, 'Sywell's victim, say rather. His victim in every way, as I will shortly tell you.' And he informed his father in detail of what Jackson had discovered from Burneck.

When he had finished his father said grimly, 'More than ever I cannot regret having disposed of such a monster—other than that I might have brought dishonour on to the family if what I had done had become known. Poor child, to think that she was living the hard life of a dressmaker's apprentice and later of Sywell's victim when, if I had known of her existence, I should have been happy to take her into my home and treat her as one of my immediate family.'

Now if only my father will tell her *that,* thought Marcus, returning to his room, all will be well and my darling will have no regrets about declaring herself a Cleeve.

'Do I look well?' Louise asked her forewoman, who was fitting her into a charmingly simple pale-blue afternoon frock designed to give off an impression of youthful innocence. Marcus was due to arrive at any moment to drive her to Berkeley Square to meet her new family.

'I am sure,' he had said, 'that you have no need to worry about your reception, you will find the warmest of welcomes waiting for you.'

He had already told Marissa and Sophia of her and they had both spoken of their new relative with all the kindness and consideration which he had expected of them. But it is all very well for him, thought Louise, for he is not the stranger who is, of all people, Sywell's widow. Never mind that I shall not acknowledge his existence, since I have formally renounced my title, but that does not alter the facts of the matter.

She was still feeling awkward, although her forewoman had assured her that she looked most *comme il faut* and fit to be presented at court when, with Marcus by her side, she was formally ushered by Cardew into Cleeve House's splendid drawing-room, where all the Earl's family were assembled. For once the Two Neds were behaving themselves, sitting demurely side by side on a sofa almost too dainty for their growing bodies.

They, together with the Earl, rose, and bowed deeply when Cardew bellowed, 'M'lord, Viscount Angmering and Miss Louise Cleeve.'

Louise blushed and looked towards Marissa and Sophia, who also rose, and offered her smaller bows. The moment they were over Marissa walked over to Louise to take her into her arms, after kissing her cheek, and murmuring into her ear, 'Oh, my dear, if only we had known of your existence we could have done so much for you. But now that you are to marry Marcus we must concentrate on making you both as happy as sandboys.'

She could not have said or done anything more calculated to put Louise at her ease. Marcus gave his stepmother a surreptitious smile: he might have known that she would turn up trumps, and Sophia, too, who said, smiling, 'I do hope that this does not mean that you will not be able to continue making my trousseau!'

'Not at all,' said Louise, 'for it is almost finished, leaving me plenty of time to make my own. They will be my swansong, you understand. In future my forewoman will run the business for me, and I shall provide any capital necessary to develop it further.'

'Excellent, my dear,' said Marissa, giving another approving smile. 'I must compliment you, Marcus, on marrying a lady with so much sound common-sense. The Yardley estates will have two splendid nonpareils running it and its future will be assured.'

The Earl, who had watched his wife and daughter take over Louise's welcome into her new family, now walked forward, saying, 'I had meant to offer you a more formal welcome, my dear, but as usual, I have been forestalled by my women! Rest assured that my pleasure on seeing you in your rightful place is as great as theirs.'

He had spent two mornings with his own, and Louise's, lawyers, examining papers and speaking to Jackson about his interview with Burneck. But it was not until the Earl actually saw Louise for the first time that any doubts about her true identity flew away.

'You are the exact image of one of my Cleeve cousins, Adelaide by name,' he said. 'You have her very look. If I had seen you on one of your previous visits when you came to fit Sophia I would have thought I was seeing a ghost—for Adelaide died in childbirth when little more than a child herself, and so she has always remained young for me.'

He did not add that he had had a *tendre* for her when he had been little older than the two Neds, but her father, who had been a great stock-breeder and improver of his sheep and cattle, had thought it unwise that cousins should marry, and they had been kept apart until she had been married off to a neighbouring squire.

Louise stared at him with great eyes and then,

before she could stop herself, she began to cry, gently and quietly. Marissa put an arm around her and said, 'Child, do not be distressed or overset. You must know how happy we are that Marcus is to marry you, and that you are restored to us.'

'I am not crying because I am sad or overset,' Louise said, through her slow tears. 'But because I am happy. No one, I do assure you, has ever said so many kind things to me in such a short time as you have done. No one has ever welcomed me so warmly. Indeed, apart from my dear friend Athene no one has ever welcomed me at all. You will think me a regular watering-pot, but believe me, I have seldom cried in the past, and hope not to do so in the future.'

She turned to Marcus and said, 'You will all think me most ungrateful for returning your kindnesses with tears.'

'No,' he said, thinking that she looked more beautiful than ever, with her eyes shining and her soft mouth quivering. 'It is most understandable. We all know that you have met with very little kindness while you were still Louise Hanslope and then Madame Félice. We will say nothing of Sywell, for he deserves nothing.'

Louise smiled through her tears at this blunt statement, so typical of Marcus. 'After that,' she said, 'I must contrive not to disgrace myself.'

'Tea!' exclaimed Marissa. 'That is what we need—and time for Louise to become used to us.

We have not even had the grace to introduce her to my Two Neds, who have been behaving in the most unusual fashion ever since you were announced. They are being so good and quiet that I fear that they may be sickening for something.'

'Pooh to that,' said Ned One cheerfully. 'It is because our tutor has been given the afternoon off so that we may join you in meeting cousin Louise. We seem to have very few relatives, so it is rather jolly to discover a new one—particularly when she is so pretty. Mark Anthony must be congratulated on his taste, as well as on his enterprise in discovering our lost cousin.'

'Oh,' said Louise, winning the two boys' hearts immediately, 'I can see that, whatever else, this particular Ned is well on his way to becoming a diplomat. Is the quiet one a diplomat, too?'

'Certainly not,' exclaimed Ned Two. 'I leave that to my senior. I wish to be a soldier, only Marcus tells me that once we have beaten the French there may not be any more wars for some time. That does not change my mind. To be a soldier and not worry about getting killed would add to the fun of wearing a uniform, not detract from it. Later on, Cousin Louise, I should like to show you my collection of toy soldiers—if Marcus can spare you, that is.'

'I should be delighted,' she told him truthfully, happy to be treated as one of the family. She had known few boys, but she could judge immediately that the Two Neds were splendid specimens of young manhood. It was already obvious that when they had gained a few more years both boys were going to be heartbreakers, whatever else they might become.

She listened with some amusement to their mother telling them both, with mock severity, to stop being frivolous, but Louise had experienced so little of such light-heartedness in her hard life that she welcomed it.

Tea, when it came, was a jolly meal, and after it the Earl asked her and Marcus to join him for some private conversation about the future.

'Angmering tells me,' he said, 'that you will be giving up your business in London and, once married, will make your home at the Abbey, when it has been improved to your taste and it is fit to live in. I have talked to my wife and we would both be most happy for you to form part of our household in Northamptonshire until you marry at Christmas—if that is what you would wish. After that I propose that, since Marcus will essentially take over the role of my retiring agent, you will live in his house until the Abbey is ready for you. After my death Jaffrey House would make a splendid residence for the Dowager Lady Yardley and the Two Neds. Such arrangements, are of course, subject to your approval.'

What could she say? With Marcus smiling happily at her, and the Earl so welcoming in his kindness, to refuse would be impossible even if she had wished to do so.

'I hardly know how to thank you,' she told him. 'Of course, I will do as you suggest—when I have wound everything up in London, that is.'

'Excellent,' said the Earl. 'Marissa is already planning your wedding, and that you should be married from the Cleeve household, as befits a member of the Cleeve family, can only add to our pleasure.'

And so it was settled. Later Marcus took Louise into the garden at the back of the house, and they had a few private moments to share their pleasure in one another's company.

'The trouble is,' groaned Marcus, after they had exchanged some hurried embraces away from the overlooking windows, 'that it is going to be deuced hard for me not to ravish you before Christmas. You grow more bewitching by the day—which shows what happiness and contentment can do to a person, I suppose—but I hardly like to tell you what it is doing to my contentment, to say nothing of my will-power.'

'So you don't mind losing your bet with Jack Perceval?' asked Louise, who was having some difficulties of her own in remaining as chaste as she ought before marriage.

'Not at all,' said Marcus. 'I had rather lose it, and gain you, than win it and not have you. I would wish that you would stand still for a moment, I have a mind to kiss you again.'

'Except that I think that we really ought to go indoors again. Your parents will be wondering what we are finding to do out of doors on a chill Autumn afternoon.'

'No, they won't,' said Marcus, with a meaningful grin. 'They will know perfectly well what we are doing—but you are right, if only because I am growing more desperate to ravish you by the minute, and much though I think that you might enjoy it, the back garden of Cleeve House is scarcely the most romantical or sensible place, to engage in such goings on.'

Reluctantly they drew apart, both wishing that Christmas—and marriage—would soon arrive, after which they could pleasure themselves to their heart's content. For the moment they would have to be happy in the knowledge that Louise, after her hard journey through life, had at last reached harbour with the man she loved—and who loved her.

Epilogue

Christmas Eve, 1812

'Oh, mam, I mean m'lady, you look like a fairy princess in that dress, indeed you do!'

Louise smiled down at her little maid, who had been translated from being her general help in Chelsea to being her personal maid since she had left London in mid-November to come and live at Jaffrey House before she married Marcus alongside Sophia and her handsome Duke. They had decided on leaving London once Louise's true identity became known, not only to society but also the Radical press.

Her sudden reappearance had, indeed, stunned society and produced enough *on dits* about her to last a lifetime. The last thing anyone wanted was that idle sensation-seekers would fill the church. Instead, the ceremony itself was to be held in the small private chapel at Jaffrey House before the bride's and groom's immediate families. Their friends and more distant relatives would attend a reception in the Great Hall. The Earl's staff and many of the faithful villagers from round about would be having a party in the kitchen after the reception was over and dancing had begun.

The only worry that Marissa and Marcus had was whether the Earl, who was daily failing, would have the strength to cope with such a demanding event.

'Nonsense!' he had exclaimed when Marissa had, cautiously, broached the subject with him. 'I would be a poor thing if I could not stand up at my children's weddings, particularly when I have spent the last ten years begging Marcus to marry.'

And so it was settled.

Rather than employ someone new to be her lady's maid, Louise had taken Mary Smith with her to Jaffrey House. Marissa's maid had instructed her in her new duties and Mary was rapidly losing her timidity and beginning to acquit herself with honour. She was already walking out with one of the footmen—and wedding bells seemed imminent.

'It's the most beautiful thing you've ever designed,' she said, adding diplomatically, 'after Lady Sophia's gown, of course.'

Louise thought that there was not a pin to choose between the two dresses. She said, a little shyly, for she was finding it difficult to believe that her time in exile was behind her and that she was really going to marry Marcus today, 'I hope that m'lord will agree with you when he sees it.'

'Oh, I'm sure he will. I don't suppose you know that Lady Yardley was very strict with him this morning. He wished to come and see you in your finery before the service, but she told him that on no account was he to do any such thing. It was bad luck, she said, and you had had enough of that already to last a lifetime. He wasn't best pleased, I can tell you, but M'lady said that seeing you were going to spend the rest of your days together, a few hours apart shouldn't be too heart-breaking for him.'

Now, wasn't that just like Marcus! The one thing she liked best about him was his positive forthrightness—so unlike her first husband's cunning evasion about everything. You always knew where you were with Marcus, whereas Sywell—and she really ought to stop thinking about him on this happy day—but for a moment she had remembered the dreadful nature of her first wedding, with Burneck standing at Sywell's shoulder and grinning away at them.

He had been invited to the party in the kitchen, Marcus had decreed, because he had turned up trumps in the end and had told the lawyers everything—even more than Jackson had wrenched out of him—so that her right to be called Louise Cleeve had been established beyond a doubt. Louise wasn't sure that she wanted him there, but Marcus's kindness was something else which she valued, so she had not argued with him.

Jaffrey House was crammed with guests: a large number from outside the county had been staying at some of the better inns, or with local landowners who had been invited to the joint weddings. Athene and Nick Cameron, together with Athene's mother, who had recently married the Duke of Inglesham, her first, and only love, had taken over the Filmers' old home. The Duke had had it renovated and improved in double quick time as an occasional refuge for him and his Duchess when London society became too much for them.

'Who would ever have believed that we should be here, having celebrated my wedding and being about to celebrate yours?' Athene had whispered to Louise when the Ingleshams and Camerons had called at Jaffrey House, the day before the wedding.

'Do you remember the many times we walked in the woods and talked about our prospects in life and our possible futures? You said to me on the last occasion on which we met before you ran away from Sywell, "I have no future—and no past, either," and now look at you! Louise Cleeve, long deprived of her inheritance, restored to it, and about to marry one of the nicest men in society—after my Nick, of course. It's better than a play, is it not? And as for my mama, words fail me, which, as you know, they rarely do.' And she looked across to where the Duchess, a smile on her pretty face, was talking eagerly to Marissa about her new and happy life. 'But she deserves all the happiness she can get.

I was always troubled that because she was so good and gentle she would remain lost in a country village for ever. It only goes to show that we never know what the next day may bring.'

'Which is fortunate,' said Louise in her quiet way. 'Because the next day is not always happy.'

'Oh, but tomorrow will be, that I do know,' said Athene in her forthright way—she was nearly as forthright as Marcus, thought Louise, amused and enlivened as she always was by her best friend.

'A double wedding cannot be other than a triumph. Inglesham says that everyone in London is furious at being deprived of the opportunity to be present, but commends your common-sense for depriving them! Nick, of course, agrees with him. By the by, have the Kinlochs been invited?'

'Invited,' said Louise, 'but they are unable to be present. Emma is breeding, is having a poor time of it and her Mama and Papa have gone to Scotland to visit her for Christmas, so they will be absent, too.'

'And thank goodness for that,' exclaimed Athene. 'But poor Emma, to have her mama inflicted on her at such a time—although Nick tells me that since she married Kinloch Mrs T's manner towards her daughter is greatly changed, and so it is to be hoped.'

'And what has Nick been saying that you quote him?' asked Athene's husband, who had come up to where they sat side by side on the sofa.

'Oh, Nick, there you are. I was telling Louise that

Mrs Tenison no longer bullies Emma so much now that she is married to a peer of the realm.'

'True,' said Nick, and the three of them, Louise remembered, chatted together about this and that— 'Because,' said Athene, 'you will have little time to spend on us when you are busy tomorrow entertaining the hordes who I understand have been invited.'

Now she gazed at the clock, and realised that she would shortly be no longer plain Louise Hanslope but fancy Louise Cleeve who was about to marry her Prince Charming. And what a comic name that was for forthright Marcus Cleeve! But it suited him because he had rescued her, and made sure that she did not have to run away before midnight, but would be waiting for him to marry her without the intervention of fairy godmothers. Nor did she have any ugly sisters nor a wicked stepmother either.

Only Marissa, who was Marcus's stepmother, and she was proving to be the mother whom she had never had. On cue, as if she had read her mind, Marissa entered, to help Mary put the final touches to Louise's toilette.

'Oh, you look ravishing,' she exclaimed, handing her a spray of Christmas roses, white chrysanthemums, winter jasmine and green Christmas ferns, tied round with a wide cream sash ending in a giant bow. 'And here is your bouquet. The gardeners collected the flowers from the hothouse for you and Sophia this morning, and my maid and I prepared them for you both.'

Impulsively Louise leaned forward and kissed her benefactress on the cheek. 'You have been so good to me,' she murmured, the tears not far away. 'I did not know such kindness existed.'

Marissa smiled at her. 'This is no time for repining,' she said. 'Marcus and Sharnbrook are already making their way to the chapel, and you must be ready to join them in a few moments, and do exactly what you did at yesterday's rehearsal. Remember that afterwards you and Sophia and your bride and groom will enter the drawing-room on either side of the Earl and will be led in by Cardew, who will announce you.'

'I know I am being silly,' Louise said, 'but how is it that it all seemed so easy yesterday, but today I am all of a quiver?'

'Oh, wedding day nervous fits are commonplace,' said Marissa, smiling again. 'I was supposed to be beyond such megrims, but when I married Marcus's father I was barely able to walk down the aisle. That—and the Earl's frail health—persuaded me that a small private ceremony at Jaffrey House might be the best thing for us all. To be married among friendly surroundings takes much of the apprehension away—at least I hope it will for you.'

It had certainly taken it away from Sophia, who was on her highest ropes, but Louise found the whole business so dazzlingly exciting that the ceremony, and the reception afterwards, passed in a dream.

Was it she who walked towards Marcus, Sharnbrook, and the waiting parson? Or was it someone else? She remembered that Marcus had never looked so handsome, that the Parson had smiled at her, that she managed to say all her lines in the right order, and if her voice had sounded strange to her, it seemed to have appeared quite normal to everyone else.

Marcus had kissed her at the end, whispering, 'Welcome, Lady Angmering, to your new title.' After that she and Marcus, Sophia and Sharnbrook walked ahead of the Earl and Countess and the rest into the Great Hall, where the other guests were waiting for them. The hall had been decorated with boughs of holly and ivy to celebrate Christmas as well as the weddings of the house of Cleeve.

A long table, piled high with food, had been laid at one end of it—the whole arrangement being rather like those in exclusive gaming hells, was Marcus's private joke to Sharnbrook. Chairs and little tables had been distributed around the walls so that the guests might have somewhere reasonably comfortable to sit.

Everyone clapped when they entered, and after the formalities were over, conversation became general, and friends who had not seen each other for many months found one another after the newly-weds had received them, and rapidly began to exchange news and views.

'I had so hoped to meet Beatrice and Harry

Ravensden,' exclaimed Lavender Brabant. 'I know that they were invited, but I gather that like Lewis's wife, Caroline, Beatrice is also breeding, and the journey here would have been too much for her.'

'Oh,' said Athene, 'they are very much in the fashion, for she is not the only one. I am beginning to think that there must be something in the air of Northamptonshire to produce such an army of babies! Jack and Olivia Denning are also unable to be present for the same reason, but I gather that there are others here who have been more fortunate, since their condition has allowed them to travel.'

'And you, Athene?' asked Lavender, her eyes alight with mischief. 'Are you one of that number?'

Athene offered her a sphinx-like smile. 'At this present moment, my dear, all that I can say is, perhaps, but I am hopeful. And you? I hear that I must congratulate you on being delivered of a book. A Flora, I believe, most apt. I shall boast about you when I go north. It is not everyone who knows an author.'

Lavender's pleasure was apparent. 'You are very kind,' she said. 'But I fear it is only a modest offering—not at all like something written by the Author of Waverley.'

'But much more useful,' returned Athene, 'only you must not tell Nick so! Being a true Scot, he is sure that no one can compare with a writer who comes from Caledonia. I need not ask if you are happy,' she added, before moving on. 'Both you and

Barnabas look like the man who lost a halfpenny
and found a half-crown! I hope to speak with him
before we leave. At present he is being cornered by
Dungarran. They are probably having a jolly coze
about Newton and numbers!'

On the contrary, as Lavender later discovered,
Barnabas had been quizzing Dungarran about the
marriage state. 'I gather,' he had just said to him,
'that you and Hester are the Romeo and Juliet of
Steepwood. How are you faring now that you are
married? Do you talk about mathematics all day and
everyday—or only on Sundays when the Parson's
sermon has been dull?'

'Not all the time,' returned Dungarran with a
straight face, before reducing the crowd about him
to happy laughter by saying, 'But I do have to tell
you that addition having been completed we are now
multiplying.'

Barnabas was, for once, a little slow in grasping
the joke, but on doing so said with a grin, 'Oh, I
suppose that you mean Hester is expecting.
Congratulations and all that.'

'Accepted,' said Dungarran with a bow, 'and I
gather that you, too, are to be felicitated, you lucky
dog. It is not everyone who acquires a vast inheritance—but I suppose that you deserve it more than
most. Looking around me, I would hazard a guess
that most of our friends and relations have much to
be pleased about.'

'Yes,' said Barnabas. 'The odd thing is that most

of our good luck seems to have occurred since Sywell's demise, but we'd better not dwell on that.'

'No, indeed,' agreed Dungarran. 'I understand that the Home Office has given up the search for his murderer, on the grounds that they are desperately short of staff, and that rather more important crimes need to be solved. After all, Sywell was no great loss.'

'True,' replied Barnabas. 'I must say that I am relieved to have heard the last of that business. So long as that shadow was hanging over us, no one connected with the wretch could be truly happy to-day.'

They were not the only persons present who touched briefly on Sywell's murder, but no one was tactless enough to mention it to Louise, or any of the Yardleys.

Louise, indeed, looking around her, Marcus's comforting presence by her side, many of her friends and acquaintances enjoying themselves before her, was starting her new life by banishing her old one to the shades.

Marissa whispered in her ear, 'You look even more radiant than you did this morning, and your deportment during the wedding ceremony was all that was perfect. You see how foolish your fears of the morning were.'

So she had not disgraced herself as she had feared, and now she could enjoy herself. Hugo Perceval was coming towards her, his wife,

Deborah, by his side, looking as radiant as Louise was beginning to feel. She must be sure to congratulate them prettily when they had congratulated her.

Alas! On their way towards her Deborah half-turned to acknowledge a friend she had just seen, and in the doing she collided with a footman carrying a trayful of glasses of champagne to the long table. Glasses and champagne cascaded to the carpet, but by great good fortune many of the glasses remained unbroken, so that the champagne missed drenching most of the surrounding guests.

Deborah looked at Hugo in dismay. He grinned, 'Things are improving, my love. Usually I am your victim, but I seem to have escaped unscathed this time.'

'Oh, Hugo, I never mean any of it to happen, you know that.' She sighed. 'It's very sad. I haven't had an accident for ages.'

'No, indeed. Not since you drove us into the duckpond shortly after our wedding,' he agreed, smiling down at her.

'What an unhandsome thing to say! That wasn't my fault,' she began indignantly. Then, with a characteristic change of mood, she said gloomily, 'What a liability I am. I don't know why you put up with me.'

Hugo laughed and raised her hand to his lips. 'Deborah, you are the delight of my life, and I adore you. I wouldn't change you for the world.'

He led her to where the Duke and Duchess of

Inglesham sat with Athene Cameron and her husband Nick in an octagonal recess away from the main noise in the room, but where they could see everything which happened. They were busily engaged in enjoying the good food and wine which the Yardleys had provided in such quantity.

Hugo said, 'Sit here, Deborah, my darling, and talk to Athene while I collect some food and wine for us. She is sure to make you laugh.'

'Now that,' said Athene, with mock severity, 'is a statement certain to doom me to conversation of such absolute dullness that all it will result in will be heavy yawning—but do fetch Deborah something nice. We can all eat, drink and be merry together.' And she pulled forward a chair for the embarrassed Deborah.

'Oh, you cannot imagine how…' Deborah began to Athene, who gave a jolly laugh in reply, saying, 'Oh, yes, I can. I tripped over my overlong court dress when I was presented to the Prince Regent. Imagine my consternation and the expression of all the flunkeys present when I ended up in a position suitable for someone who wished to kiss his feet. Now that is true embarrassment.'

'Are you funning me, to make me feel better,' asked Deborah doubtfully.

'Indeed not. That is all perfectly true, is it not, Nick?'

'Yes,' nodded Nick. 'The only person present not overset was the Regent himself, who said, ''The spectacle of a pretty woman prostrate before one is a sight to delight Princes is it not?'' And then he offered her his hand to enable her to rise. More than that, her popularity was ensured when she did so without apology and offered him a grand curtsey before moving on.'

Hugo returned with 'enough fodder to feed a regiment', as he informed them cheerfully, to find his wife chattering animatedly away, all her hesitant and apologetic manner quite gone.

Of course, as Nick and the Duchess well knew, the whole Prince Regent farrago was a total myth designed by kind Athene, and adroitly supported by her husband, to put poor Deborah at ease, and in that it certainly succeeded. Louise, meanwhile, might have lost Deborah and Hugo to talk to, but she had gained Dungarran and Hester, who were invited by the Earl to join them at the separate table before the empty hearth where the main wedding party was about to be served.

Once seated, Dungarran leaned over towards Marcus, saying cheerfully, 'I was never so surprised in my life as when I received an invitation to your wedding, Angmering. Some fellow named Jack Perceval who claims to be a distant relative of mine—with what justice I don't know—said that he had a bet with you that you would not be married before the year was out. He took you on—and here you are—well and truly hitched. Was there any truth in his claim or was it just a silly *on dit?*'

Marcus, with one rueful eye on Louise, said, 'Yes, indeed, and willy-nilly I paid Perceval his winnings when I lost my bet. Not that it was a major sum, mind you, but even if it had been, once I met my wife, I knew I was going to have to cough up. What's money compared with winning a peerless woman?'

'What indeed! But I have to inform you that, charming and clever though your wife is, she is not peerless so long as my Hester is in the running for such a title.'

'To say nothing of my Sophia,' quipped Sharnbrook, breaching etiquette by kissing his bride on her cheek. 'If there are any peerless stakes being run she is sure to be a prime candidate!'

'There speak three happily married men,' said the Earl, who had been listening to what his son had got up to with some amusement. 'I thought that you never gambled, Angmering, but now I know differently.'

'Ah, well, sir,' said Marcus with a grin. 'I only did so that night because I was half-cut and miserable—unusual states for me, you will agree.'

'That is true,' admitted his father. At which point Ned Two leaned forward and said, 'I thought that you never got drunk, Marcus. What a horrid bad example you do set to the pair of us, eh, Ned One? I shan't listen to another of your lectures about *our* bad behaviour after hearing that.'

'Now, boys,' said their mother. 'You are not to

be impertinent towards your brother on his wedding day.'

Ned One, from his position down the table, said, 'Does that mean that we can be impertinent towards him on all other days, Mama?'

'Oh, I can see that we have a future logic-chopping lawyer here,' said Dungarran, laughing. 'A Lord Chief Justice, no less.'

Ned One shook his head vigorously, 'Indeed not, sir. Marcus told us that you are a noted mathematician, and that is what I intend to be when I leave Oxford. Perhaps you could give me some advice on the matter, after luncheon is over.'

'Well, if I can't,' said Dungarran, raising his glass in Ned One's direction, 'then Hester will. I am the more pedantic of the pair of us, and she is the more original—a regular female Pascal.'

Hester, thus called on, engaged in mock reproof of her husband. 'Now Dungarran,' she said. 'Behave yourself. You make me sound fearsome, but no matter, I shall be only too happy to help Ned with his maths.'

This lively and light exchange set the tone for the table's conversation. Louise, who was already dazed by the mere fact of being married, was quite overcome by the cheerful banter which went on around her. She had never before been a member of a happy family party, and so she whispered into Marcus's ear.

'Are they always like this?' she ended.

'Usually,' said Marcus. 'But particularly so today, when they can see how happy Sophia and I are.'

'Truly,' said Louise, who could scarcely believe that she had finally arrived in what seemed to her an earthly paradise. Oh, she was not foolish enough to believe that there would be no unforeseen pitfalls in her future life, but to someone who had always been ignored, exploited, overlooked and neglected they would be as nothing compared with what she had experienced in the past.

Toasts were exchanged, and she soon began to understand that if she were not to end up under the table she must only take a sip of her wine at each tribute which was offered to her. The noise in the room grew—and that, too, was a new experience for her.

Marcus saw that she was becoming not so much weary as bewildered by all that was going on around her. When the syllabub at the end of the meal was served, he whispered to her, 'After we have eaten our dessert, we must rise and tour the room making our formal farewells to our guests. Then the musicians will enter once the remains of our meal are cleared away and you and I, Sharnbrook and Sophia will lead the first dance before leaving. The celebrations will go on long after our departure.'

Secretly Louise was relieved to hear this. She was enjoying herself, but she wanted to be alone with Marcus as soon as possible—and she knew that Sophia felt the same about being with Sharnbrook.

They were not leaving Jaffrey House, but would retire to a suite of rooms there, while she and Marcus would drive to the land agent's house near the Abbey. It had been made ready for them to live in until the Abbey had been repaired, redecorated and provided with new furniture, all fit for the heir to an Earldom to enjoy.

Touring the room was a happy event, though. Everyone was smiling, everyone seemed to be as happy as they were. Athene said to her, her voice low, 'I can only wish you as fortunate as I am with Nick. I like your Marcus. He seems a sterling fellow and everything which you deserve in life.'

'Oh, he is,' said Louise fervently. 'And I am so happy for you, too.'

The last persons to whom they said farewell were the Earl and Marissa. If the Earl looked even more frail than usual, his pleasure at seeing his son happily married was so evident that it overshadowed their fears for him. Marissa, of course, wished them all the best, and the Two Neds were as irrepressibly naughty as usual.

After that the newly-weds visited the kitchens where the servants were busy laying out their own banquet, and the butler led the toasting to their future happiness.

Once they were in the entrance hall with the doors open while they waited for their chaise to be brought round, Louise, her bouquet in her hand, was astonished to see that it was still daylight, and said so.

'Which,' returned Marcus, 'is not surprising, seeing that it is only two thirty on a fine, if cold, December afternoon. I must say,' he added, 'that I am glad to be alone with you at last. My face has grown quite stiff from smiling at people and making small talk. Not my thing at all.'

'Nor mine, either,' agreed Louise, 'which is ungrateful of me, I know, since everyone seemed genuinely happy to see us married.'

'Particularly my father,' said Marcus. 'He thought that I would remain a bachelor, turning in due time into one of those old men who sit in London clubs grumbling that everything is going to the dogs!'

Their chaise finally arrived on the gravel sweep, and before they were helped into it, Louise turned to Marcus and said, 'I trust that you have not forgotten to inform the coachman of our first destination.'

'No, I made quite sure that he will not take us straight home. I see that you still have your bouquet with you.'

'Yes. Sophia threw hers into the room before we left, and it was caught by one of Dungarran's sisters.'

Marcus laughed and kissed her before they set off, saying, 'I assume that she's yet another mathematician in that family, since Ned One was so taken by her that he could not stop talking to her. By the by, when we stop will you be warm enough in what you are wearing, or shall I help you into your pelisse before we leave the chaise?'

'Please,' said Louise, and then lay back, silent, watching Marcus, still scarcely able to believe that she was actually married to him.

'The only thing which I ask of you,' he said, leaning forward to take her hand in his, and looking deep into her eyes, 'is that we do not take too long over your mission, since I have been in a truly wretched state ever since the Parson pronounced us man and wife. If I don't get you into bed with me soon I'm fearful that I shall need a doctor to minister to me before we get there.'

'Oh, I think that I can provide you with all the necessary ministrations when we do arrive there,' said Louise naughtily.

'Hope deferred maketh the heart sick,' quoted Marcus mournfully.

'On the contrary,' returned Louise, 'the old adage has it that "Desires are nourished by delays."'

They both laughed together, and Marcus remarked, 'It is fortunate that most proverbs and old sayings contradict one another, thus providing us with a contest which neither of us can win.'

'And, seeing that it is our wedding day, that is a most excellent thing,' was Louise's answer to that.

They were still laughing when the coach stopped at the edge of the wood in which the Sacred Grove stood. Louise took off her pretty white kid slippers and exchanged them for a pair of stout shoes which they had brought with them. The shoes which Marcus had worn to be married in were stout enough for him to walk on the path through the wood. The day was moving towards its close, the sun was riding behind a cloud and the dark wood lay before them.

'Fortunate it is,' she said to Marcus, after the footman helped them down, 'that it is a fine day, even if a little gloomy now.'

'Our first walk as a married pair,' said Marcus. 'Take my arm, Lady Angmering.'

'Willingly, Lord Angmering,' she replied, and they strolled along the path towards the heart of the wood, passing from light into dark as the trees clustered nearer and nearer together. They fell silent, for there seemed something almost mystic about their journey which compelled a holy quiet. Finally they reached the Grove and the rune stone which stood in its centre.

'There,' said Louise, as she had done in Marcus's dream. 'I wish to go there,' and she pointed to the stone.

Facing it was an iron bench, placed there by some long-gone Earl of Yardley. Marcus had brought a blanket with him, which he spread on its seat before they sat down.

After they had remained silent for a short time, he asked her, 'Now, Lady Angmering, tell me why you wished to come here and why you have brought your bouquet with you.'

'Because…because Athene and I often visited the Grove and tried to imagine what the people were like who carved the runes on the stone and called it Sacred. We both knew of the legend: that the pagans who built it cursed all those who might come after and who would not worship the stone as they ought. The curse said that the new owners of it would not prosper—and who is to say that the curse was not effective? Think only of the Dissolution of the Monasteries, the ruin of the Abbey, and after that the unhappy lives of the Cleeves, Earls of Yardley, who took over Steepwood, until they lost the Abbey to Sywell—and then remember how horrible his end was. Now we shall inherit them both: the land and the curse.

'The gypsy fortune teller told us that she had lifted the curse on us, so perhaps we shall be safe, but I wish to see it lifted for everyone who comes after us. I don't like to think of our descendants inheriting unhappiness and ruin, and so I want the curse to end once and for all. That is why I asked you to bring me here today, and why I brought my bouquet. I want to lay it before the rune stone, and tell it, and its attendant spirit, that we honour the men who erected it, and the women who lived with them. That being so, we beg them of their mercy to lift the curse, so that the Cleeves, and those who might come after them, may live and die as ordinary people, not as those doomed. Do you think me foolish, Marcus?' she ended.

'No, my dear,' he said, 'never foolish. Besides, it cannot hurt to try to exorcise the curse. Lay your flowers before it, and say your prayer.'

Louise rose. She knelt before the stone, regardless of what it might do to her finery, and placed the bouquet between herself and the side of the stone with the runes carved on it.

'Accept this offering of my wedding bouquet,' she said. 'We honour those who made you, and beg most humbly that since we also honour the spirit of the stone, you lift the curse not only from us, but from our children. We beg you to send us a sign that you have accepted my offering so that we may not see them, or their children's children doomed to unhappiness.'

She put her hands together as if in prayer, and knelt there for a little time before beginning to rise.

Even as she did so, the sun broke through and a ray of the purest light, the first of the day, streamed out to illuminate the stone and the bouquet which lay before it.

'A sign,' Louise breathed. 'A very sign.'

She turned towards Marcus, holding out her hands to him. He took them, then swept her into his arms to kiss her on the lips, not with the passion which he was later to display, but with reverence.

'Sign or not,' he said, 'I commend you for what you have done. And now, Lady Angmering, let us go home and bless our marriage in the time-honoured way.'

'Yes,' she said, and they walked towards their waiting coach, and to the happy future which lay before them, their children, and their children's children.

* * * * *

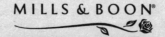

Three brand-new,
sinfully scandalous short stories

Regency
BRIDES

Anne Gracie, Gayle Wilson, Nicola Cornick

Available from 20th September 2002

*Available at most branches of WH Smith,
Tesco, Martins, Borders, Eason, Sainsbury's
and most good paperback bookshops.*

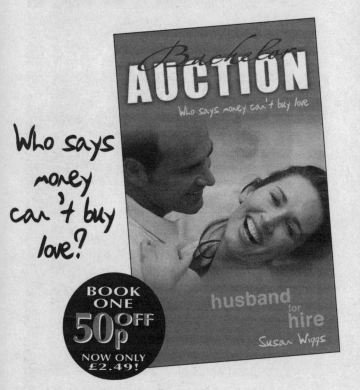

Do you think you can write a Mills & Boon novel?

Then this is your chance!

We're looking for sensational new authors to write for the Modern Romance™ series!

Could you transport readers into a world of provocative, tantalizing romantic excitement? These compelling modern fantasies capture the drama and intensity of a powerful, sensual love affair. The stories portray spirited, independent heroines and irresistible heroes in international settings. The conflict between these characters should be balanced by a developing romance that may include explicit lovemaking.

What should you do next?

To submit a manuscript [complete manuscript 55,000 words]
OR
For more information on writing novels for Modern Romance™

Please write to :-
Editorial Department, Harlequin Mills & Boon Ltd, Eton House, 18-24 Paradise Road, Richmond, Surrey, TW9 1SR or visit our website at **www.millsandboon.co.uk**

Modern Romance...
"seduction and passion guaranteed"

Submissions to:
Harlequin Mills & Boon Editorial Department,
Eton House, 18-24 Paradise Road, Richmond, Surrey, TW9 1SR,
United Kingdom.